SHORT STORIES:

London in
two-and-a-half dimensions

CJ Lim + Ed Liu

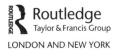

Routledge
Taylor & Francis Group

LONDON AND NEW YORK

First published 2011
by Routledge
2 Park Square, Milton Park, Abingdon, Oxfordshire, OX14 4RN

Simultaneously published in the USA and Canada
by Routledge
711 Third Avenue, New York, NY 10017

Routledge is an imprint of the Taylor & Francis Group, an informa business

Printed and bound in the UK by Ashford Colour Press Ltd

British Library Cataloguing in Publication Data
A catalogue record for this book is available from the British Library

Library of Congress Cataloging-in-Publication Data
Lim, C. J.
Short stories : London in two-and-a-half dimensions / C.J. Lim and Ed Liu.
p. cm.
1. Lim, C. J.--Themes, motives. 2. Liu, Ed--Themes, motives. 3. London
(England)--In art. I. Liu, Ed. II. Title. III. Title: London in two-and-a-half
dimensions.
N6797.L46A4 2011
720.22'2421--dc22
2010047311

ISBN13: 978-0-415-66889-7 (hbk)
ISBN13: 978-0-415-57358-0 (pbk)

Contents

Preface

The modern age has been an unkind chapter in the history of narrative architecture. In pre-secular times, it was not unusual for buildings to be constructed of and around narrative – the proportions, alignment, size and decoration of the great Egyptian temples and tombs were determined by metaphor, not utility, while the Doge's Palace in Venice, with its Bridge of Sighs, Porta della Carta (Document Gate), Scala dei Giganti (Giant's Stairwell) and winged lions, is as much an assemblage of anecdotal vignettes as building. Circular and cruciform plan forms, once steeped in mystical and religious significance, are now merely unfashionable shapes. Today's built environment presents such a poor receptacle for story that Arata Isozaki felt compelled to publish drawings of his

Tsukuba Centre in Tokyo as ruins, immediately after its completion in 1983, in order to imbue it with a fictional life beyond the building's conventional existence.

Roland Barthes comments in 'Introduction to the Structural Analysis of Narratives' that 'narrative is present in every age, in every place, in every society; it begins with the very history of mankind and there nowhere is nor has been a people without narrative. All classes, all human groups, have their narratives, enjoyment of which is often shared by men with different, even opposing, cultural backgrounds. Caring nothing for the division between good and bad literature, narrative is international, transhistorical, transcultural: it is simply there, like life itself.'[1] It is therefore significant that buildings, as physical repositories of and monuments to human culture, now rarely signify anything beyond their quotidian function.

Using the techniques of collage, the ten 'short stories' that follow investigate the reinvestment of narrative form in architecture, depicting a London that is peopled with both real and fictional elements from a variety of sources. In the acquisitive nature of collage, the thematic intent of this book appropriates ideas, tropes and characters from pre-existing critical thinking in the fields of architectural representation and narrative structure.

The Architect as Storyteller

Current forms of architectural representation reveal a dichotomy
of purpose. The primary form of architectural drawing, produced
by the majority of professionals in practice, still follows the triadic
system of plan, section and elevation. While these orthogonal forms
of representation are well suited to the task of relaying information
for construction or fabrication purposes, they possess no qualitative
or phenomenological intelligence. That is not to say that they do
not describe and proscribe the occupation of space – Robin Evans
points out that 'if anything is described by an architectural plan,
it is the nature of human relationships, since the elements whose
trace it records – walls, doors, windows and stairs – are employed
first to divide and then selectively to re-unite inhabited space.'[2]
Nonetheless, the codification of construction drawings is designed
to prevent ambiguity or multiple interpretation by using a strict and
abstract system of notation. Walter Benjamin goes so far to say that
'the most essential characteristic of the architectural drawing is
that it does not take a pictorial detour.'[3]

The early deconstructivist paintings of Zaha Hadid or the
Chamberworks drawings of Daniel Libeskind exploring the
parallels between music and architecture, tell a different story. As
Lebbeus Woods comments, drawing is a mode of thinking: 'there

are ideas and feelings that can only be expressed in drawn form. We might imagine, if we look at the caves of Lascaux, that drawing came before writing and was, in its narrative making of marks, its source.'[4]

What both types of architectural representation have in common, and what distinguishes them from a fine art drawing of a building, is that the subjects constitute a projected future. Whether that future is realized or not is not necessarily significant in this respect. Evans comments, 'Drawing in architecture is not done after nature, but prior to construction; it is not so much produced by reflection on the reality outside the drawing, as productive of a reality that will end up outside the drawing.'[5]

The key point established is the conjectural nature of architectural drawing – an alternative future patterning of space and its occupation is advanced that, due to the real potential for its reification and the contextual surroundings, cannot be considered wholly fictive. In the case of more fantastical propositions where there is no intention of realization, divergence from the status quo is magnified with a concomitant inflation of the proposition's fictive quotient. On the one hand, this might lead us to question the legitimacy and place of 'paper architecture', on the other, a case could be made that the breadth of the disjunction frees us to consider changes in spatial practice that could be truly transformative.

Geoff Manaugh, futurist and author of BLDGBLOG, is convinced of architecture's narrative potential: 'architecture, as a discipline, can itself be used to tell stories. In fact, some of the most interesting student work today comes complete with elaborate plots and story lines, supplied for no other reason than to explain why a particular building should exist or require designing. These stories very often exceed today's mass market fiction in imaginative strength.'[6]

Regrettably, the most common vehicle of architectural conjecture is the computer render; produced for mass consumption, the photorealistic image is capable of reaching and convincing a wide audience of a proposition's validity. Its strength, however, is also its weakness – so plausible is the image at simulating reality that no 'reading' or interpretation of the architecture is required or demanded. In its own way, it is as much a fait accompli as the architecture it represents, frozen in time against a perfect and eternal blue sky. As Neil Leach writes in 'The Anaesthetics of Architecture', 'the intoxication of the aesthetic leads to an aesthetics of intoxication, and a consequent lowering of critical awareness. What results is a culture of mindless consumption, where there is no longer any possibility of meaningful discourse.'[7]

Drawing and modelling, whether physical or virtual, are not the only means of representation available to the architect. Text is an often-overlooked tool in the description of architectural propositions and when used, tends towards the explicative rather than the expressive. The written word is usually limited to specification and the justification of design decisions rather than contributing to creative or conceptual design. An exception to this tendency is the giving of names to buildings, either formally by architects and developers, or informally by the general public. Sobriquets such as 'The Shard', 'Falling Water' and 'The Flatiron Building' are powerfully suggestive, ascribing meaning and qualities that may or may not be espoused in the architecture that they are projected on.

The prima facie reason why architecture and narrative are considered irreconcilable is that buildings do not unfold over time in the way that films or novels do. Space nevertheless contains temporal associations, most obviously in the architectural promenade in which spaces gradually reveal themselves to a mobile observer. Architecture also has the capacity to transcend the physical, encoding poetic sequences into its fabric – the Danteum, Terragni's rewriting of 'The Divine Comedy' in architectural form, for example, does more than illustrate Dante's work; it translates the poem's structure and metre into spatial proposition. The question is also not necessarily how to inculcate architecture or architectural representation with temporal elements; a rapprochement can be equally reached by viewing conventional narrative in less sequential terms, focussing more on the descriptive than the prescriptive.

The Storyteller as Architect

The city as protagonist appears periodically in literature and film. Noir, for example, has become almost synonymous with Los Angeles and the writings of Chandler, Cain and Ellroy. 'Berlin: Symphony of a Great City', the German silent film of 1927 directed by Walter Ruttman, portrays a day in the life of the German capital. As a medium with intrinsic chronological progression, film lends itself easily to plot structure, yet there is no strong narrative thread to the city symphony, perhaps to maintain the focus on the city itself, rather than its inhabitants. Instead, Ruttman links themes and perspectives using Soviet montage techniques, suggesting spatial connexions that would be impossible in a conventional narrative.

Peter Ackroyd classifies his magnum opus on London as a biography, insisting that we should regard the city as 'a human shape with its own laws of life and growth'. Like Ruttman, Ackroyd elects not to follow a chronological sequence in London's story: 'Contemporary theorists have suggested that linear time is itself a figment of the human imagination, but London has already anticipated their conclusions. There are many different forms of time in the city, and it would be foolish of me to change its character for the sake of creating a conventional narrative.'[8] Similarly, in 'Invisible Cities', Italo Calvino avoids a conventional sequential structure in his paeon to the city of Venice, playing out the prose poem through a series of urban descriptions recounted to the Kublai Khan by the explorer Marco Polo. When asked by the Khan whether he will repeat the same tales to his people, Calvino echoes Barthes, explaining that there are as many versions of a tale as there are listeners, via the proxy of Polo: '"I speak and I speak," Marco says, "but the listener retains only the words he is expecting ... it is not the voice that commands the story: it is the ear."'[9]

Other authors have used architecture as a framework for their stories, the most obvious example being George Perec's 'Life: A User's Manual'[10] which uses the device of an imaginary Parisian apartment block, 11 Rue Simon-Crubellier, to structure his work; Perec pictures the building with its façade removed, behind which there are ninety-nine rooms set out in a ten by ten grid, each of which is designated a chapter describing the stories of the rooms' inhabitants in connexion with a central puzzle.

Like any other character in a novel, architecture assumes the role of protagonist when the plot of a story is unable to unfold without its intervention. The cathedral of Notre Dame, for example, is key to a number of episodes in the life of Quasimodo – the hunchback is first introduced as a child at the cathedral's foundlings' bed; he becomes deaf after being made Notre Dame's bell ringer, claims sanctuary at the top of the bell tower on behalf of the gypsy girl Esmerelda, and finally takes refuge within its massive stone walls when besieged by a mob intent on his death.

The Fallacies of Linearity

The creation of a building is generally perceived as a linear process. Appraisal of a client's needs is followed by the development of a brief; a concept is then established, around which a design evolves though drawing and modelling. Soon after, the principal intentions described in the drawings and models become frozen as technical and contractual considerations assume prominence, culminating in an inhabitable structure via the agency of a builder. The brief is the beginning, the design the middle and the building the end. However, it is equally valid, and indeed commonplace, for brief to follow building, for instance when extant urban fabric is repurposed to house new functions, or for design to precede brief, for example in the case of the geodesic dome. Design is by nature iterative; beginnings and ends are found where we choose to locate them. As the postmodern author Neil Gaiman observes, 'human beings like things to be story-shaped. The universe does not hand over beginnings, middles, endings; stories cut and shape the world, impose patterns on it.'[11]

The linearity of the building is also challenged by Beatriz Colomina, who contends that the physical building is just one of many possible modes of architectural representation. She argues that the site of architectural production has moved from the built environment to other media such as film, photography and journalism, a 'displacement that presupposes a new sense of space, one defined by images rather than walls'.[12] Drawings, specifications, photographs, models and texts all are manifestations of a single platonic archetype, and any one of these manifestations is as representative of the architecture as the physical building.

In other fields, the dismantling of sequential narrative as dogma is well established, perhaps illustrated most viscerally in the cut-ups and fold-ins of William Burroughs and Brion Gysin. Inspired by Dada experiments of the 1920s, Burroughs and Gysin applied the techniques of collage to text. Burroughs describes the cut-up method thus: 'Take a page. Like this page. Now cut down the middle and cross the middle. You have four sections: 1 2 3 4 ... one two three four. Now rearrange the sections placing section four with section one and section two with section three. And you have a new page. Sometimes it says much the same thing. Sometimes something quite different.'[13] The cut-up technique is a potent rejection of linearity, demonstrating how the juxtaposition of aleatory elements can lead to original and surprisingly coherent outcomes relying on imagery and poetic association. However, the rare instances of recombinant epiphany derive their potency from an obligatory mass of barren white noise, leading Burroughs to employ cut-ups only as an intermediary stage of composition in his later work rather than in their unexpurgated form.

The Reader Reborn

In 1967, Roland Barthes' landmark essay, 'The Death of the Author', declared the independency of a text from its author, empowering the reader to distill a unique and personal reading from a multiplicity of layers and meanings: 'We know now that a text is not a line of words releasing a single "theological" meaning (the "message" of the Author-God) but a multi-dimensional space in which a variety of writings, none of them original, blend and clash. The text is a tissue of quotations drawn from the innumerable centres of culture.'[14] The liberation of a work from an authoritative voice has proved to be double-edged. As a society, we have become accustomed to having information spoon-fed to us, and for culture to entertain rather than inform – film has become synonymous with the 'high concept' movie in which a story's premise can be condensed into a single tagline, while the novel has been reduced to the 'unputdownable' beach read. Consequently, we have lost the patience and facility to develop a critical understanding of a work with any intended ambiguity or invested subtext.

This cultural drift is even more pronounced in the field of architecture where perception of a building rarely extends beyond its superficial appearance. With the disappearance of signified meaning in contemporary buildings and the obsolescence of meaning in buildings of antiquity, our ability to read architecture has completely atrophied, if we are in fact aware that architecture can be read at all. Despite the rich imaginative conjecture that thrives in schools of architecture, the intention to implant buildings with meaning is increasingly uncommon. When it does occur, it is often the equivalent to the high concept movie, exemplified by projects such as Libeskind's Manchester Imperial War Museum in which the building is composed of three interlocking shards that seemingly derive from a shattered globe – a seductive opening statement but, at the same time, a one-liner.

In an urban milieu where context and the genius loci of a place have become subsidiary to economic and political considerations, reducing architecture to pre-determined programmes and their formal manifestation, the act of binding architecture into the story of its inhabitants can only bring a new relevancy to the built environment, projecting, but not predicating, the rules of its occupation.

The short stories of this book's title are set in different time periods of London, intentionally locating themselves in the liminal territory between fiction and architecture to provoke an engagement between readers and their two-dimensional counterparts occupying the depicted city. The stories are neither illustrated texts nor captioned images; the collages represent a network of spatial relationships, and the text, which splices genres such as science fiction, magical realism and the fairy tale, a thread that links some of the nodes of that network together. The written elements of each piece begin to cast a rigid carapace around the amorphous field of potential stories generated by the collages, but should be regarded as merely one reading of them. Text and collage, or more precisely, text and photographs of collage, are two aspects of a story existing in a troubled relationship, sometimes working in parallel with one another, sometimes reinforcing one another and other times contradicting one another.

A Romance of Many Dimensions

In his eponymous novella, Edwin A Abbott created the two-dimensional world of Flatland,[15] whose inhabitants consist of lines, points and polygons. Subtitled 'a romance of many dimensions', Abbott's story, written in 1884, is both a mathematical treatise on dimensional perception and a satire examining Victorian sexuality and the class system. Taking a cue from this work, each of the stories in this book begins life as a two-dimensional sheet of paper. The paper and is then cut, inscribed, folded and fused into a narrative, occupying a territory that is both real and surreal; cardboard cut-outs are spliced and woven into yarns with shadowy nuance to partially occupy the third dimension. Using paper, carbon and glue as ingredients, the stories construct a sequence of improbable marriages between reality and fantasy, laced with a healthy dose of myth and locational specificity – a leather-bound suitcase masquerades as a living breathing house with cooing hens perched on window sills, a dating agency at Battersea brings prospective owners together with their ideal pet, three towers in Smithfield Market built from straw, sticks and bricks form a porcine dormitory for meat packers. Like the artwork described in Abbott's Victorian satire, the short stories are 'immoral, licentious, anarchical and unscientific' yet, from an aesthetic point of view, 'glorious', 'ravishing' and 'a pleasure to behold'.

Collage has been chosen for this work to take advantage of the medium's inherent plurality – pieces of a collage or assemblage are only ever half-assumed into their new context, bringing with them a wealth of connoted meaning from their original time and place. We usually expect objects to exist in a singular location, but the elements in a collage or assemblage oscillate between existences like Schrödinger's Cat, presenting a flexible vessel in which the reader is encouraged to deposit his or her own historical and cultural montage.

The ultimate purpose of this book is to demonstrate that architectural representation need not be a neutral tool or mere picture of a future building, that drawings and models have a direct influence on the conceptual development of a project and the generation of form, and that there are alternatives to the reductive working methods of contemporary architectural practice.

NOTES

1. R Barthes, 'Introduction to the Structural Analysis of Narratives' in 'Image Music Text', trans. S Heath, Fontana Press, London, 1977, p. 79

2. R Evans, 'Figures, Doors and Passages' in 'Translations from Drawing to Building and other Essays', Architectural Association, London, 1997, p. 56

3. W Benjamin and T Y Levin, 'Rigorous Study of Art', Vol. 47, October 1988

4. L Woods, 'Line', an entry on the Lebbeus Woods Blog, [http://lebbeuswoods.wordpress.com/2008/05/05/line/], retrieved 05 September 2010

5. R Evans, 'AA Files', Annals of the Architectural Association School of Architecture, No.12, Summer, 1986, p. 7

6. G Manaugh, 'The BLDGBLOG Book', Chronicle Books, San Francisco, 2009, p. 17, 19

7. N Leach, 'The Anaesthetics of Architecture', The MIT Press, Cambridge, MA, 1999, p. viii

8. P Ackroyd, 'London: The Biography', Vintage, London, 2001, p. 2

9. I Calvino, 'Invisible Cities', trans. W Weaver, Harcourt Brace & Company, New York, 1974, p. 135

10. G Perec, 'Life: A User's Manual,' trans. D Bellos, Harvill Press, London, 1996

11. N Gaiman, interviewed by P Nayar, 'Business Times', Singapore, 8 July 2009

12. B Colomina, 'Privacy and Publicity: Modern Architecture as Mass Media', The MIT Press, Cambridge, MA, 1996

13. W S Burroughs and B Gysin, 'The Cut-up Method of Brion Gysin', in Thomas Parkinson, 'A Casebook on the Beat', Cromwell, New York, 1961, p. 105–106

14. R Barthes, 'The Death of the Author' in 'Image Music Text', trans. S Heath, Fontana Press, London, 1977, p. 146

15. E A Abbott, 'Flatland', Dover Publications Inc., New York, 1992

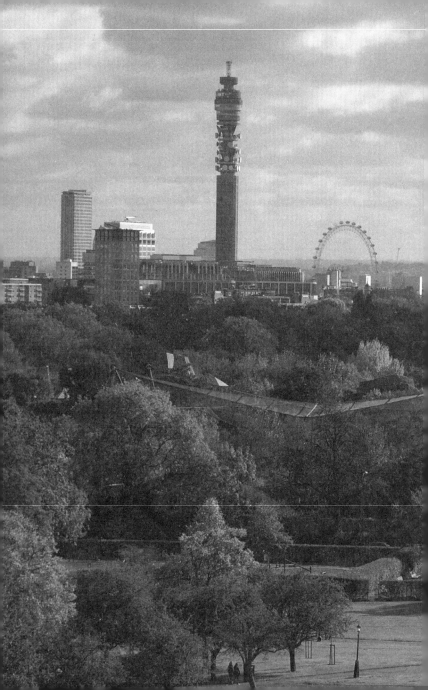

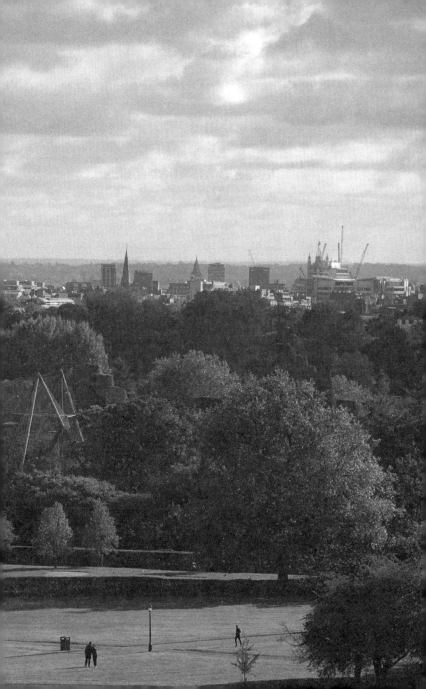

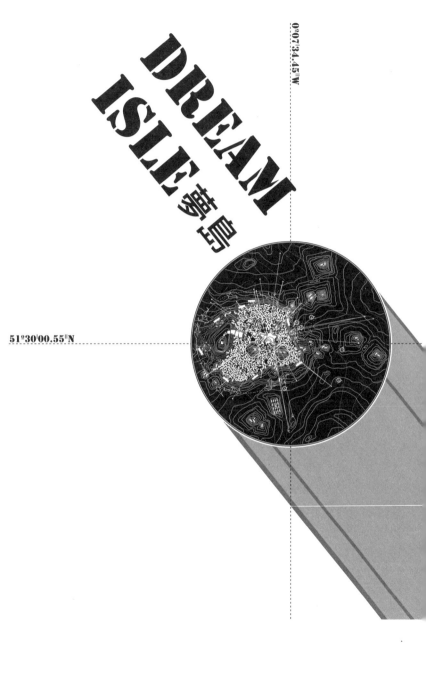

0°07'34.45"W

DREAM
ISLE 夢島

51°30'00.55"N

PROLOGUE
Dream Isle

Prologue

London is a city and cities are alive. They breathe, they grow, they spawn, they die and they dream. This is London's dream.

Feeding on the memories of its visitors and cosmopolitan populace, London's dreams traverse icons such as St Paul's Cathedral, the Houses of Parliament, Primrose Hill, Trafalgar Square and the green courts of Wimbledon, but not as we know them. In these dreams, the city is protagonist, and this is how it sees itself.

Causality and reason drift through the gargantuan proscenium windows of Buckingham Palace and across the roving kaleidoscope of the realm's ancient mounds of tea and baked sponge. The denizens of the Dream Isle comprise puffed-up swans borne on palanquins and an anarchic monarchy circled by MPs (appropriately dressed in shark costumes), while a skein of magpies unfurls the British Museum, daily revealing their hoard of sequestered treasure.

Dreams, like cities, shape us and are shaped by us. Architects would have us believe that the edifices that make up the city are immutable and solid, monuments to their designers' immortality. They are not. In both London's imaginings and reality, landmarks and events assume shifting magnitude and significance, constructing distorted maps of desire and experience. Narrative obeys no logic as London searches for an ever-changing identity imprinted by its waking life. Time, scale and relationships become fluid, and the city is forever on the brink of the strangely familiar and the familiarly strange.

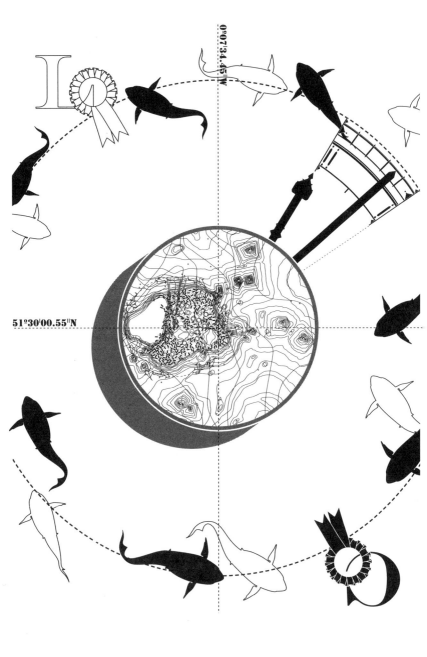

0º07'34.45"W

51º30'00.55"N

HOUSES OF PARLIAMENT

The laws of the land are debated and decreed at the Palace of Westminster where the two Houses of the Parliament, the House of Lords and the House of Commons, meet.

Two red lines, just over two sword lengths apart, are inscribed on the floor of the House of Commons. Protocol dictates that Members may not cross these lines when Parliament is in session, preventing debate from degenerating into duel. Today, swords may no longer be worn inside the Palace, and a loop of ribbon in the cloakrooms is reserved for each Member of Parliament for the storage of weapons. Members may not address each other by name and are obliged to use the monikers 'my honourable friend' or 'honourable lady/gentleman'.

The shallow waters around the Dream Isle are hazardous – sharks in the guise of MPs, Tory Blue and Labour Red, circle each other warily, ever vigilant of the slightest vulnerability or slip of tongue. These pitiable predators are condemned to an eternal cycle of attack and counter, never reaching a conclusion, other than the occasional feeding frenzy when one succumbs to age or to scandal.

0°07'34.45"W

51°30'00.55"N

THE WHISPERING GALLERY OF ST PAUL'S CATHEDRAL

In the 16th Century the main thoroughfares of the city, built in timber and plaster, would act as echo chambers giving rise to a unique 'London Sound'. The murmuring of the city would intensify in different pockets of London, reaching its apotheosis in the whispering gallery of Wren's masterwork. Running around the interior of the dome of St Paul's, ninety-nine feet above the cathedral floor, a whisper against its wall is audible to a listener with an ear held to the wall at any other point around the gallery.

London's soliloquy resonates within colossal teacups embedded in the island's spongy earth. The susurration is composed from an amalgam of tongues, drawing on words from one dialect that make no sense in another. If a listener spoke every language from every era, perhaps the secrets of the city would be revealed.

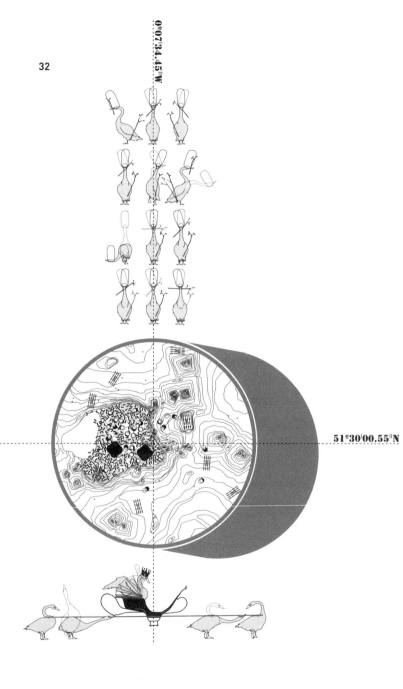

0º07'34.45"W

51º30'00.55"N

THE CHANGING OF THE GUARD

The mute swan, 'Cygnus olor', was introduced to Britain around the 12th Century as a prized bird for the table. Since that time, the reigning monarch has been entitled to claim ownership of any unmarked swan swimming in open water. Every year in late July when parent birds are moulting and cygnets are still too young to fly, the birds are rounded up during the Swan Upping and identified by the Queen's swan marker by order of the crown. Dressed in uniform and travelling in six traditional wooden skiffs, the swan uppers circle a bevy of swans and converge on the brood with the cry 'all-up!'

The Monarch and the royal palaces have been protected by the Household Troops since 1660 and the Changing of the Guard still takes place at Buckingham Palace at half-past-eleven in the morning. When the Queen is in residence, there are four sentries; when she is away there are two. The soldiers are drawn from one of the five regiments of foot guards in the British Army.

WIMBLEDON & THE BRITISH MUSEUM

The All England Lawn Tennis Club in Wimbledon hosts the world's premier tennis tournament at the end of June each year. Rain stopping play during Wimbledon fortnight has become as much an institution at SW19 as strawberries and cream – the groundskeepers of the rye grass courts furl and unfurl the rain covers in tune with the capricious movement of black skies overhead. The pigeon population at the All England Club has dramatically declined in response to an increase in the number of hawks and trained marksmen. Magpie numbers in the area are, however, on the rise.

The European magpie, 'Pica pica', appears frequently in European folklore, known for its tendency to steal and horde shiny objects. According to tradition, one should pinch oneself as if in a dream on sight of a lone magpie to ward off ill fortune. Like other members of the corvidae family, magpies become attached to particular nesting grounds, and are portents of doom should they abandon them.

The British Museum is a universal museum holding an encyclopaedic collection of material from across the world and all periods of human culture and history. For the benefit of its audience now and in the future, the Museum is committed to sustaining and improving its collection. The Museum deplores the looting of antiquities with the ensuing damage to archaeological sites and loss of cultural context. The Museum does not acquire objects that are known to result from such looting.

At this particular moment on the Dream Isle, the British Museum and the grass courts of Wimbledon have fused into a hybrid entity, coming into being through the aid of a tidings of magpies. As grey clouds threaten, a thousand black and white feathered stewards, tethered to the perimeter of a folded grass tarpaulin, take flight and open out a canopy to protect the hoard of artefacts and treasures they have accumulated since 1753.

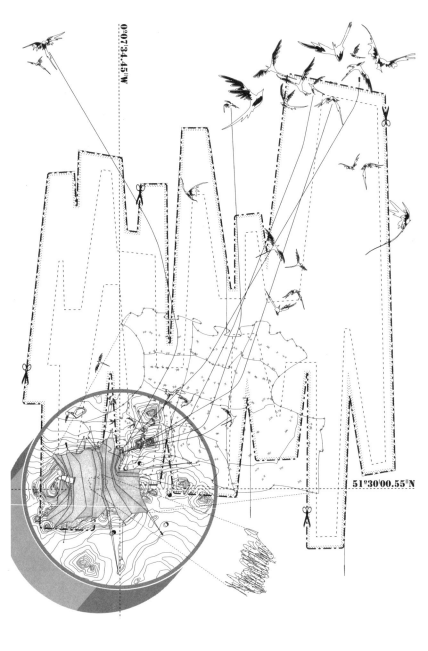

0°07'34.45"W

51°30'00.55"N

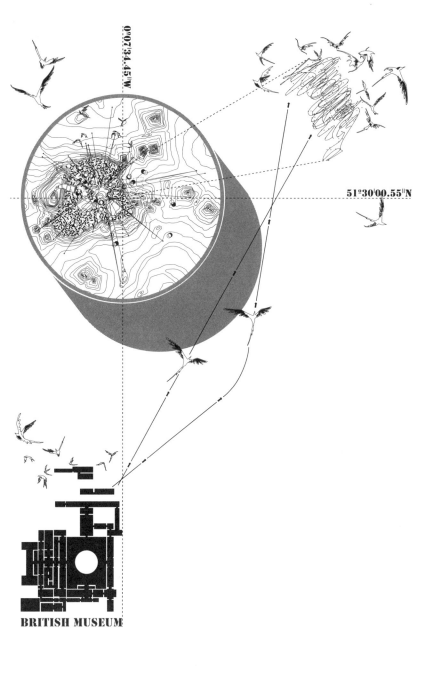

0°07'34.45"W

51°30'00.55"N

BRITISH MUSEUM

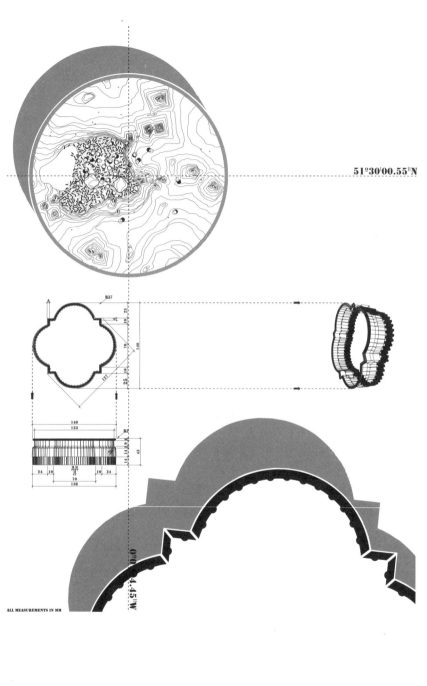

51°30'00.55"N

R37

140

140
133

43

24 10 10 24
70
138

ALL MEASUREMENTS IN MM

TRAFALGAR SQUARE

This is the largest square in London and has been a meeting place since the Middle Ages. Set within it are the Jellicoe and Beatty Memorial fountains, positioned to break up and control crowd surges during riots. Designed by Sir Charles Barry and erected in 1845, the original granite basin walls are quatrefoil combined with a square in plan.

A symmetrical shape that forms the overall outline of four partially overlapping circles of the same diameter, the quatrefoil is an old Christian motif that recurs throughout London's history, stamping its distinctive form cookie-cutter like, from Medieval times through to the 21st Century, on Gothic churches, military decoration and shortbread tins.

0°07'34.45"W

IX

V

51°30'00.55"N

BANK

The bowler hat, pin striped suit and umbrella remain universal signifiers of the faceless London City 'Gent'. The bowler hat is nowadays seldom seen, but the treadmill existence of the faceless city worker has proliferated exponentially to colonize the four million square metres of land that were dropped into London's commercial heart in the 1980s.

Swans in bowler hats feed the insatiable machine that is the most advanced and elaborate foreign exchange in the world. A perpetual motion machine in the form of a gargantuan waterwheel spanning between the quatrefoil fountains of Jellicoe and Beatty completes a revolution every twenty-four hours, delivering the worker swans from home to work and back again.

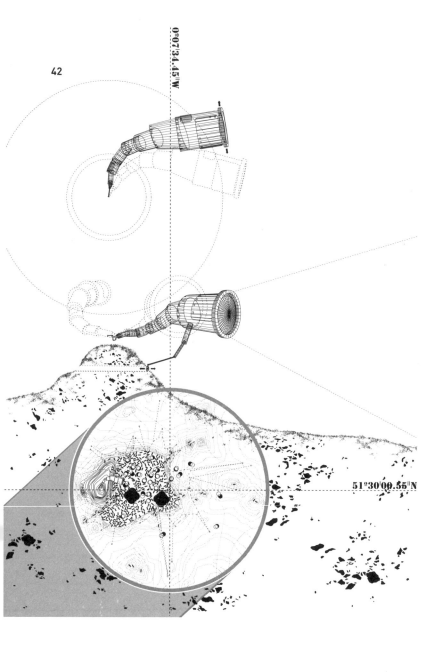

51°30'00.55"N

PRIMROSE HILL

At a height of 256 feet (78 m), Primrose Hill forms part of an elevated region known as the 'northern heights' lying between the smaller eminences running from London's north in a north-westerly direction. At the hill's apex at the north end of Regent's Park, there is a small plateau at the confluence of several footpaths where the viewer experiences the London panorama in more detail than from any other location. The kaleidoscopic view takes in Trellick Tower to the west and Canary Wharf to the east.

As such, the tyrannical gaze of Primrose Hill wields great influence on the shape of London, shackling its natural growth. The vistas to the Cathedral of St Paul and the Palace of Westminster are determined by geometrical definition, slicing two conical voids through the city that no man-made edifice may encroach.

Primrose Hill manifests itself on the Dream Isle as a roving telescopic contraption mounted on a promontory of air-filled Victoria sponge. Watched through this kaleidoscopic lens, the Isle takes the form of a giant glass petri dish, its components jockeying like bacterial cultures for dominance, continuously shifting scale and morphing into one another.

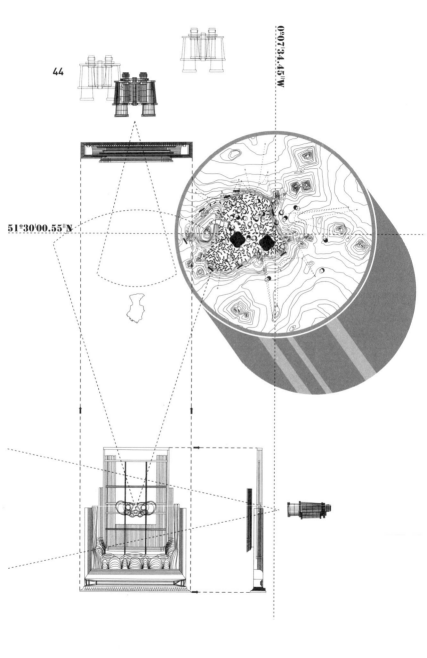

44

51°30'00.55"N

0°07'34.45"W

BUCKINGHAM PALACE

The 775 rooms of Buckingham Palace have served as the official London residence of Britain's sovereigns since 1837. The Throne Room is dominated by a proscenium arch supported by a pair of winged figures of 'victory' holding garlands above the 'chairs of state'.

The British Royal Family is the world's most famous family. The British tabloids are the world's most powerful press. The relationship between these two formidable institutions is symbiotic – the Windsors help the press sell newspapers in return for their celebrity, stature and power, simultaneously satisfying the public's voracious appetite for scandal and voyeurism.

The fenestration of the Palace appears on the Dream Isle as colossal proscenium arches – or perhaps the rest of London is miniaturized, it is impossible to tell. The arches are not windows onto the world, but windows onto the Palace, where the Royal Family, unwittingly or otherwise, stage the world's favourite soap opera and original reality show.

0º07'34.45"W

T

E

A

51º30'00.55"N

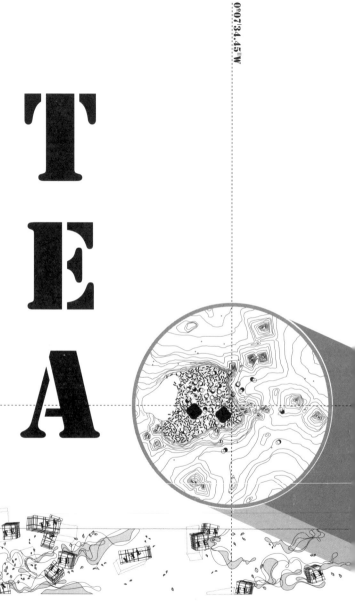

EAST INDIA DOCKS

The history of London, built on the fruits of colonial trade as much as clay and chalk, is entwined with the history of tea. Of the bountiful merchandise from both eastern and western civilizations that would cross paths at the East India Docks, tea was the most significant. The bedrock of London, the national beverage began as an expensive and fashionable pastime, leading to London's suburban tea gardens that became bywords for hedonism and depravity.

The British East India Company, which gives its name to the docks, was virtually an independent imperial power with its own army, policies and governance. The monopoly of the company culminated in the Tea Act of 1773 and the Boston Tea Party in which 342 crates (45 tonnes) of fine loose-leaf tea were jettisoned from the company's ships the 'Dartmouth', 'Eleanor' and 'Beaver' into Boston Harbour by individuals dubiously clothed in Native Mohawk dress.

In the autumn of 1774, the flotsam and jetsam of 45 tonnes of tea drifted across the Atlantic, gradually accumulating at 51° 30' 00.55" N, 0° 07' 34.45" W.

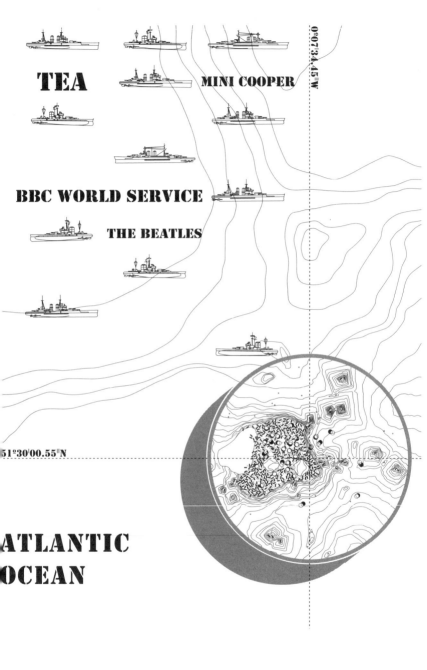

TEA

MINI COOPER

BBC WORLD SERVICE

THE BEATLES

0°07'34.45"W

51°30'00.55"N

ATLANTIC
OCEAN

NEW BRITTANIA

The Second British Empire came into being when Great Albion dispensed with the sword and took up the pen. Invading the world by culture instead of military might, the BBC World Service and the Beatles floated out across the airwaves, the Mini Cooper became a cinematic star, and Messieurs Lipton and Twining appropriated tea from the Orient and sold it back as a symbol of Britain.

London's mental picture of the world is a perfectly circular flat disc. In this world, London lies at the epicentre, its unique spirit rippling out and transforming every outcrop it touches before spilling over the edge into the ether. In time, as with all things, the well will run dry, whereupon London shall re-imagine itself again, replenishing the source that will nurture future empires.

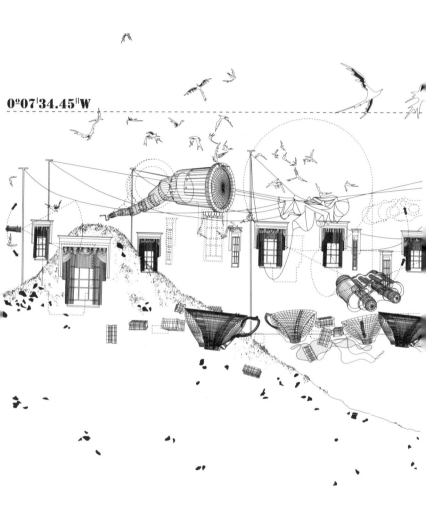

0º07'34.45"W

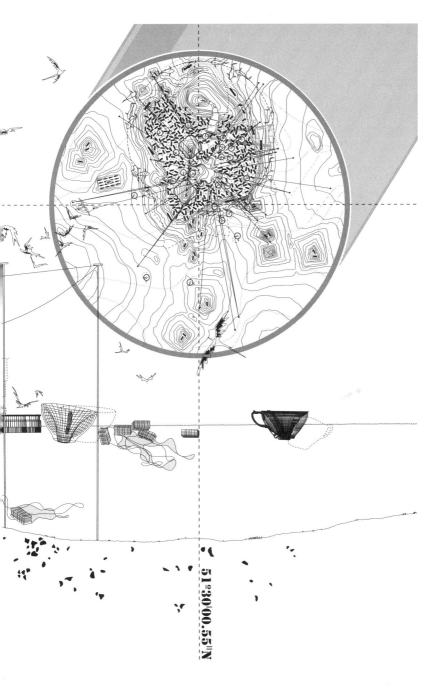

51°30'00.55"N

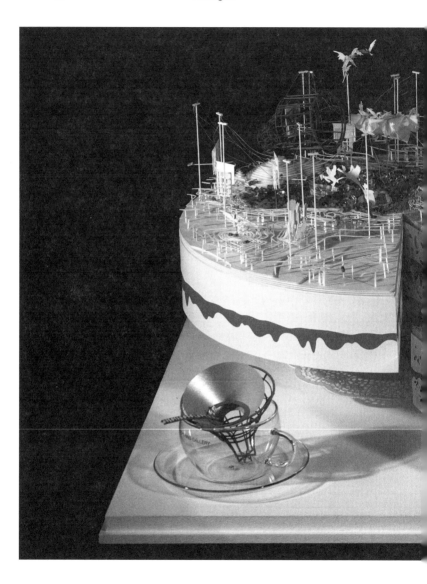

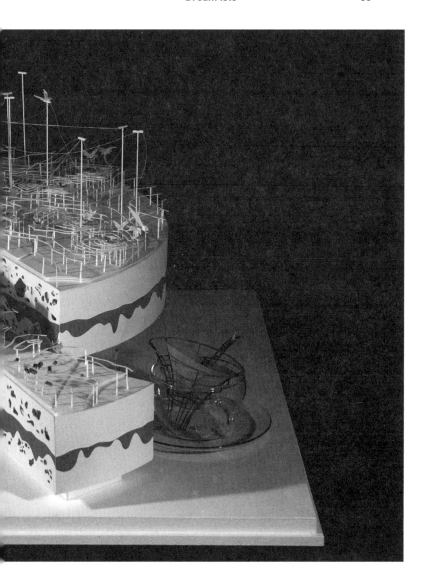

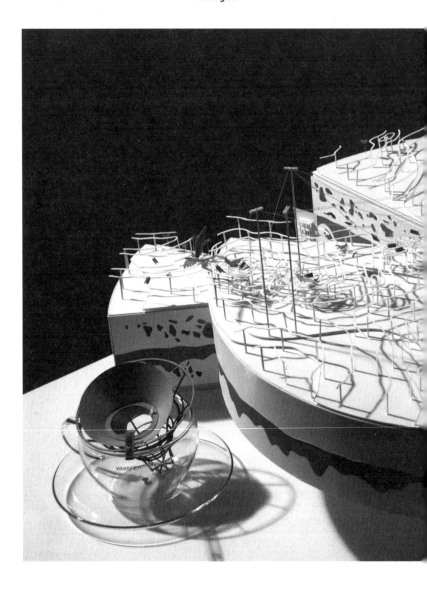

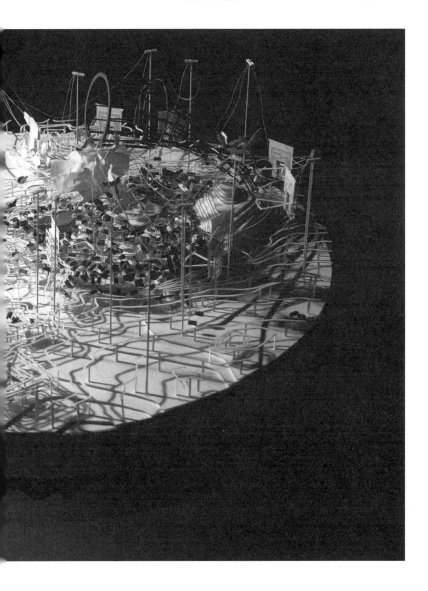

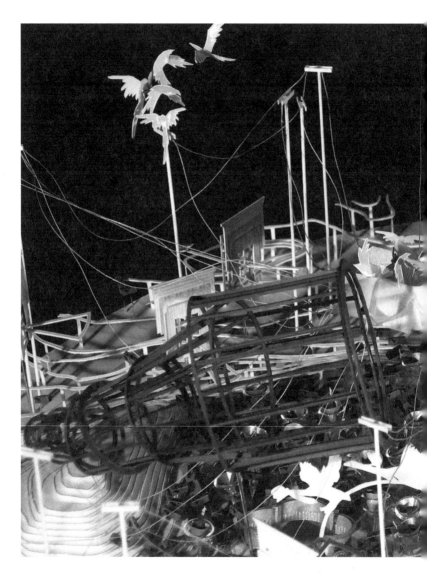

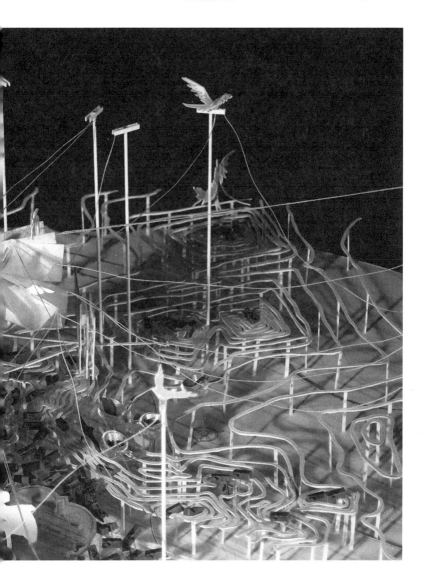

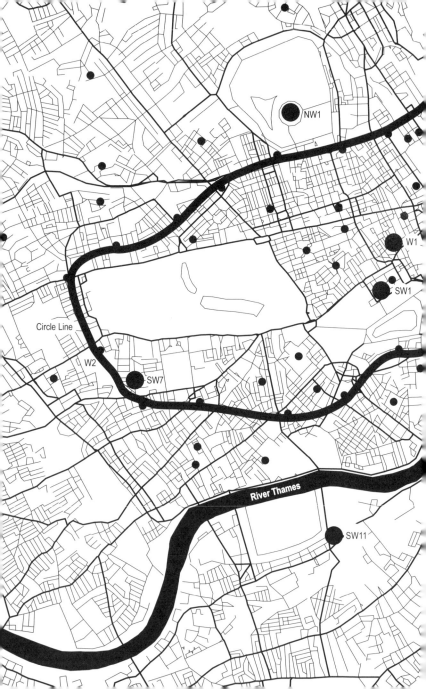

NW1

W1

SW1

Circle Line

W2

SW7

River Thames

SW11

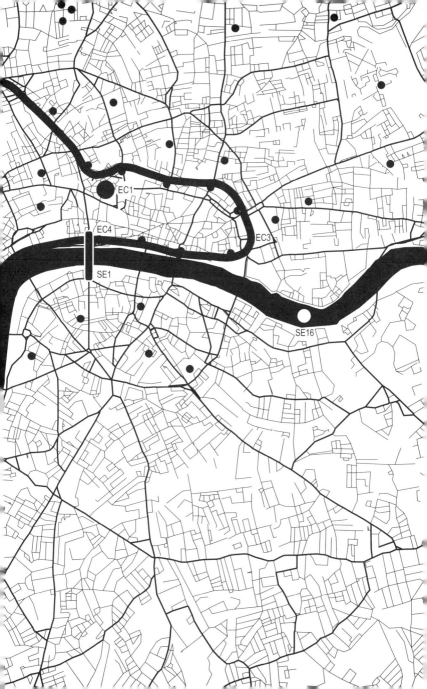

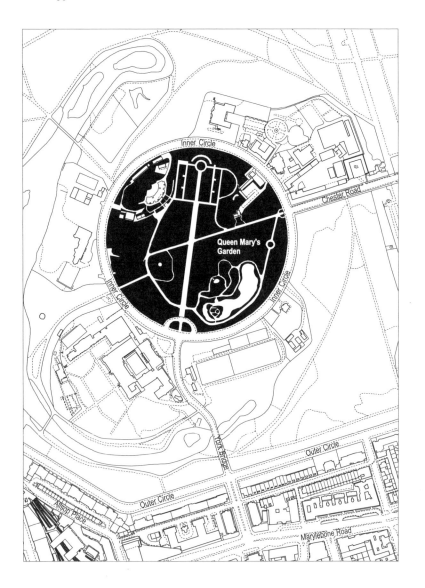

N W 1

A Midsummer Night's Dream

A Midsummer Night's Dream

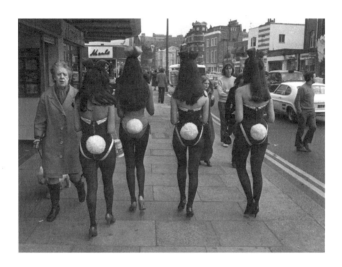

Welcome to the world of Playboy! You can take great pride in being selected as a Bunny; it's a job that you will find is both unique and exciting. The Playboy Bunny has created a new definition and standard for charm, beauty and friendly service. Playboy Clubs are world-famous for their distinctive décor, unique facilities, good food, man-sized drinks and, particularly, their beautiful Bunnies. To guarantee the high standards which our keyholders have come to expect, we are extremely selective in our Bunny hiring procedures ...

... mingling by any female employee with any patron or guest is not allowed and shall be cause for immediate dismissal. Bunnies may, however, converse briefly with patrons, provided the conversation is limited to a polite exchange of pleasantries and information about the Playboy Club. A bunny may never, under any circumstances, divulge personal information about herself or other Bunnies such as what they do outside the Club, last names, phone numbers, addresses, etc. Bunnies may:

1. have their pictures taken with patrons, provided there is no physical contact whatsoever;

2. dance with patrons at the feature dance party, provided there is no close physical contact, (twist, watusi, bugaloo, etc., are examples of acceptable dances).

- 'The Playboy Bunny Manual', Detroit Training Booklet, 1968

Jessica straightened her ears and checked her cottontail in the mirror. Her collar, bow tie and cuffs were not crooked and she had her flashlight and lighter on her person. Her hair elegantly coiffed and face made-up, she went to report to Regina, her Bunny Mother, for an appearance inspection and weighing, determined that she would receive no demerits today. Working the Midsummer Night's Dream Party would earn her five merit points, leaving her just twenty shy of claiming a well-earned £8 bonus.

Somebody had taken the interior of the Playboy mansion, transported it into the heart of London's royal parkland and then pulled away the floor.

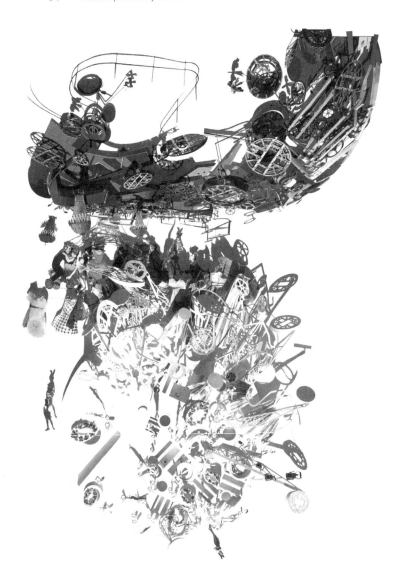

Private events were normally a chore, but Jessica would have gotten on her hands and knees to wait at the Midsummer Night's Dream Party. Besides the generous tips she could expect, she had heard on the grapevine that the Bond actor Sean Connery and footballer Georgie Best would be amongst the celebrities in attendance. This year, for the first time, Playboy's flagship annual party on the first Saturday of August was to be held outside America. London was the obvious choice; the club at Park Lane with its gambling revenue had almost single-handedly kept the Playboy empire afloat. Located opposite Hyde Park, the 'Hutch on the Park' spanned five floors, representing a money-spinning enterprise for its owners and a pleasurable distraction for its patrons.

A student of English literature at Westfield College, Jessica was teased mercilessly by her fellow Bunnies for being squarer than square; she was the last person they might have imagined working at the club. The irony was that behind the costume and coquettish façade, she had never behaved more properly; as a Bunny, she was bound by strict rules to mind her Ps and Qs, to refrain from wearing any jewellery and to decline any alcohol. Only lemonade or pop was permitted, but even then, only out of sight of guests.

Jessica was savvy and self-aware enough to understand that Hugh

Gravity-defying silk curtains, along with trompe l'oeil divans and gilt mirrors, formed a hallucinatory backdrop for the night's entertainments.

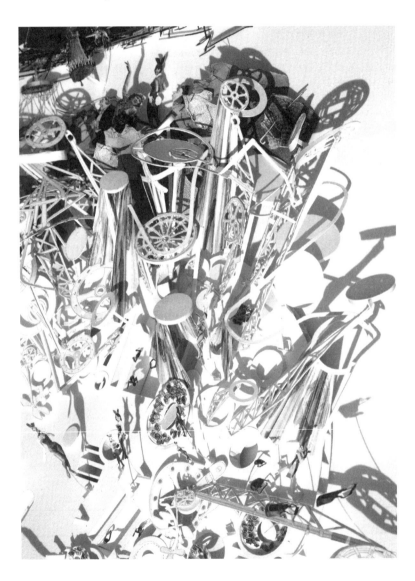

Hefner had changed the public's perception of sexual desire over the years. He and Victor, his right-hand man in London, were trading in the fantasy of carnal pleasure rather than the pleasure itself, a distinction that was clear in Jessica's mind. But where the 60s was the decade of dreams, this was the decade of turning those dreams into reality. The aspirational world of the debonair male that Hugh had peddled so persuasively had helped shape the western world's new permissiveness, making adult entertainment socially acceptable, respectable even. Now, though, Playboy was in danger of being eclipsed by tawdry Soho establishments such as the Raymond Revue Bar and the Windmill Club with its nude tableaux vivants that featured static naked girls to circumvent censorship laws. Paradoxically, the seedy clip joints and walk-ups around Brewer Street provided sexual gratification that the Playboy clubs were too upright and tasteful to provide.

Victor, according to Regina, was confident that the party would revive the Playboy empire's fortunes. The plan to import the Playboy mansion to British shores for one night was an ambitious and costly undertaking but would move the Playboy lifestyle out of closed-door clubs and into a new public arena. What better venue then, than Queen Mary's Gardens, the Inner Circle of Regents Park, named in honour of the consort of George V? St John's Lodge, designed by the architect John Raffield and later extended by Charles Barry, was

The furnishings compartmentalized
the open-air space into a surreal blend
of parlour and woodland.

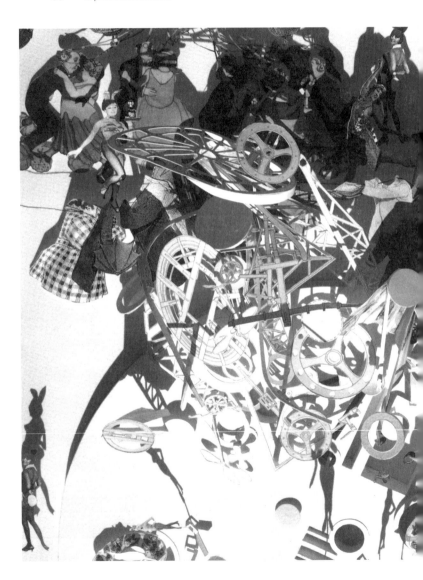

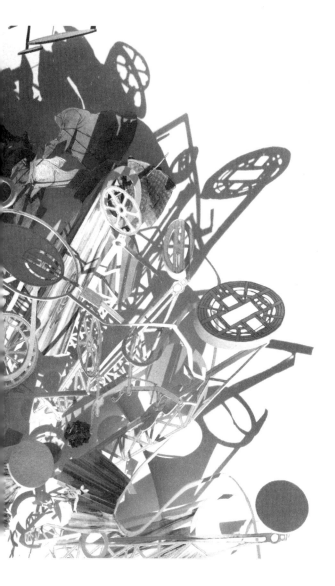

At the heart of the landscape was a shrine to the rose, the universal symbol of passion sacred to Isis, Aphrodite and Venus.

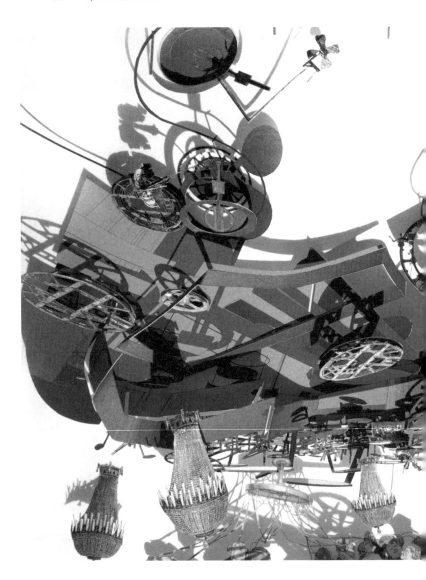

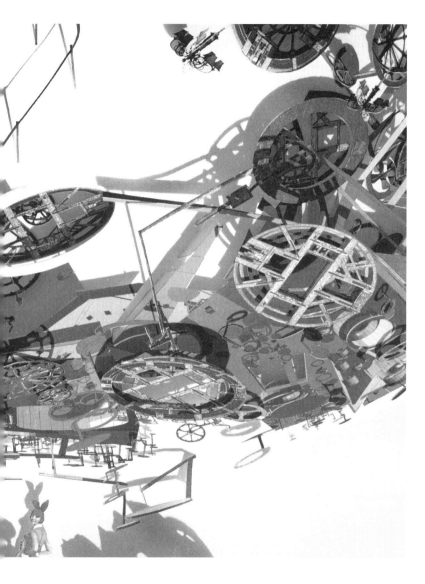

Underground chambers, replicating the hole through which Alice follows the white rabbit, had been scattered through the garden.

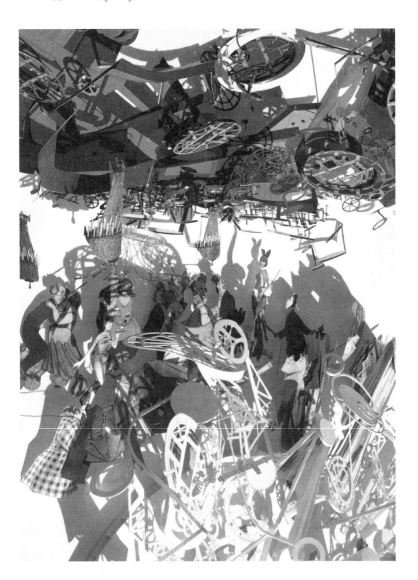

one of the few villas of the original fifty planned for the park actually built. It would dwarf the Faux Gothic-Tudor mansion in California in size and grandeur, while the waterfalls, ponds and fountains of the gardens would make an impressive substitute for the permanent mansion's pool and grotto once the water had been cleaned and heaters installed.

The theme of this year's Midsummer Night's Dream party was 'Alice's Adventures in Wonderland'. If anything could be said of Hugh Hefner, thought Jessica, he was a born storyteller. From his carefully constructed persona of louche sophisticate in silk pyjamas and monogrammed slippers to his themed parties, he was a virtuoso at spinning a yarn. Coincidentally, Jessica had attended a performance of the play, a mainstay of the open-air theatre's annual programme, at Queen Mary's Gardens just a fortnight ago. Shakespeare's romantic comedy, featuring a marriage between a Duke and a Queen, eloping lovers, a magical love potion and a fairy kingdom, could not be better suited for the park's setting.

After the site induction, Jessica went for a walk through the grounds to familiarize herself with the table arrangements. As she did so, she began to see the statues of the garden in an entirely different light. One by one, she encountered the goatherd's daughter, Hylas the Argonaut stolen away by the Nymph of Spring, and finally Triton

Jessica mused to herself whether the assemblage could correctly be called an architectural folly.

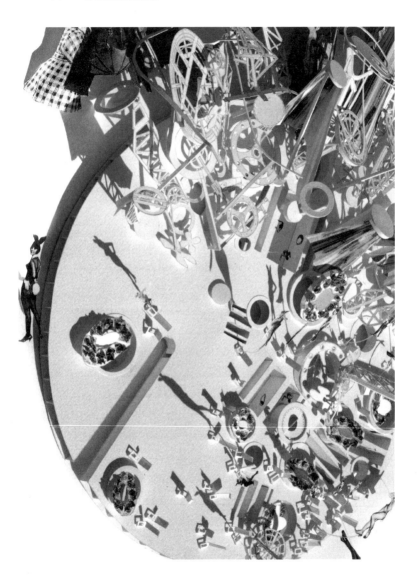

of the fountain, the messenger god of the sea, blowing his conch with two mermaids writhing at his feet. With its bronze sculptures, brimming with myth and suggestion, the Garden was already an adult wonderland, wanting only for appropriately minded visitors.

That was not to say that the designers had not done their work – underground chambers, replicating the hole through which Alice follows the white rabbit, had been scattered through the garden, capped with circular lenses and mirrors over their entrances to magnify and distort a sybaritic netherworld. Wooden flamingos dotted the garden in readiness for games of croquet while gravity-defying silk curtains, along with trompe l'oeil divans and gilt mirrors, formed a hallucinatory backdrop for the night's entertainments. It was almost as if somebody had taken the interior of the Playboy mansion, transported it into the heart of London's royal parkland and then pulled away the floor like a tablecloth, leaving the place settings undisturbed. Jessica mused to herself whether the assemblage could correctly be called an architectural folly; certainly the curtains and furnishings were parts of a building and there was no discernible purpose to them, but they were quite unlike the oriental pagodas or miniature turrets one might expect in the grounds of a stately home. What the exterior designers had succeeded in doing, however, was to compartmentalize the open-air space into a surreal blend of parlour and woodland.

The Garden was already an adult wonderland, wanting only for appropriately minded visitors.

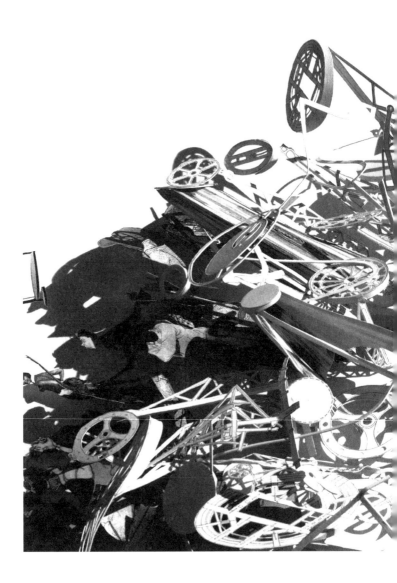

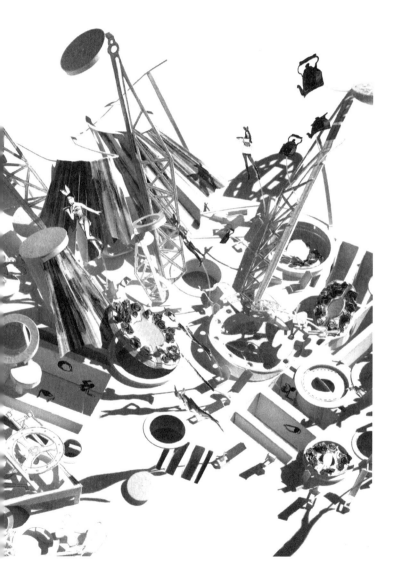

Roses in the Inner Circle belonged
to two Queens, Queen Mary and the
Queen of Hearts.

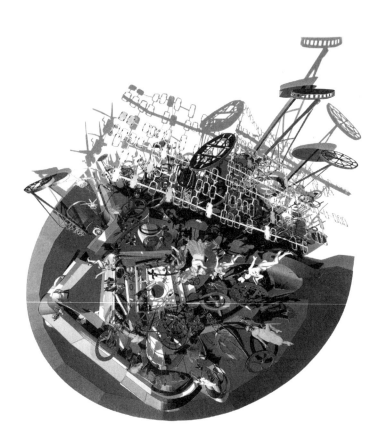

At the heart of the landscape was, rather fittingly, the Rose Garden, a shrine to the rose, the universal symbol of passion and sacred to the triumvirate of Love Goddesses Isis, Aphrodite and Venus. This day though, the roses in the Inner Circle belonged not to Gods but to two Queens, Queen Mary and the Queen of Hearts, and in deference to the latter, flowers that were not naturally red had been cowled in crimson damask hoods. The allusion and symbolism was not lost on Jessica, an avatar of Playboy's long-eared totem for the evening. Alice as a bored little girl lured down a hole by a white rabbit was not a great leap from the Playboy Bunny providing discerning gentlemen with an evening's giddy diversion. Jessica knew that she would soon be politely rebuffing the advances of intoxicated guests like a female hare in March fending off overzealous males at the start of the breeding season.

At six o'clock, for it is always six o'clock in Wonderland, the entrances to the Inner Circle closed, leaving only the grand iron and gilded Jubilee Gates for access. Dressed as hatters and hares, the guests began to arrive, and the Bunnies set about their evening's duties.

As the celebrities and guests enjoyed their tea party where bottles of wine were labelled 'DRINK ME', and cakes were iced with the letters 'EAT ME', the music began to play. Live entertainment

Playmates were frolicking in the water features while hatters and hares cavorted around them.

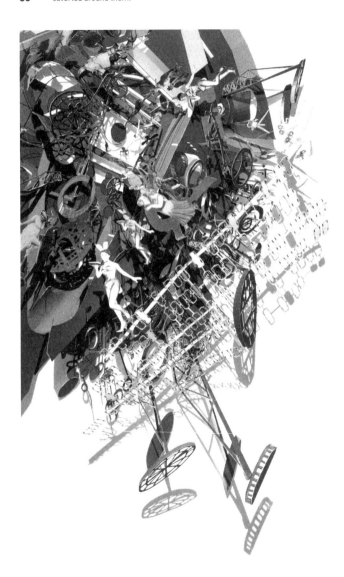

tonight was being provided by the Divine Miss M. Flown over from Hollywood and dressed as the Queen of Hearts, she delivered a lush rendition of 'Do You Want to Dance' and 'Boogie Woogie Bugle Boy' to thunderous acclaim.

Jessica was astonished at how the character of a place could be transformed purely through the comportment of its occupants. She had visited Queen Mary's Gardens in the past on Sunday mornings, drinking in the genteel landscape of rambling roses, hedges and cascading water. Now, Playmates were frolicking in the water features while hatters and hares cavorted around them chasing the figurative tail. Within the space of a few short hours, the regal gardens of Queen Mary had become unrecognizable as the evening descended into a bacchanal of wild abandon.

But all dreams come to an end, whether they belong to Jessica, Alice or poor Bottom. The guests gradually disperse and, behind the scenes, Jessica and her fellow waitresses turn in their bar cheques and rub aching muscles after a long night of Bunny Perching and Bunny Dipping. Jessica changes into jeans and slacks, deposits her costume with the wardrobe mistress, and slowly makes her way home.

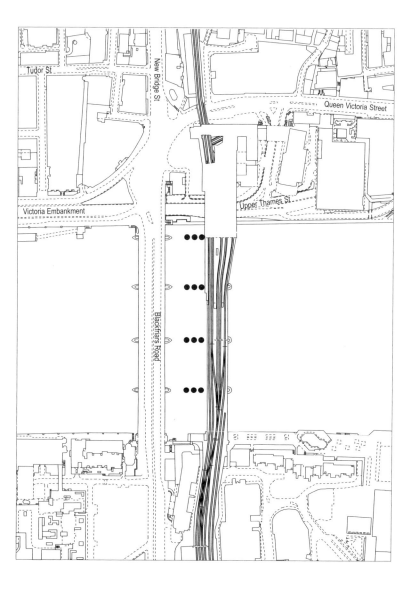

S E 1 t o E C 4

Discontinuous Cities

Discontinuous Cities

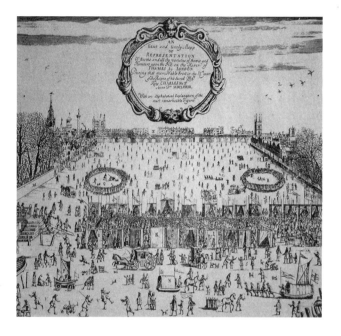

The great river cleaves the metropolis into two halves, separating its inhabitants into two proud self-proclaimed tribes. Divided not by creed, race or language, it is unlikely that a visitor would be able to discern one from the other. Indeed, a native from the south might fail to recognize one from the north or vice versa, but if the origins of one of them were to be disclosed, their differences would become immediately apparent and magnified.

When the city was in its infancy, the river served to separate two warring tribes, but after generations of peaceful migration and interbreeding, the principal root of sectarian differences has become one merely of geography. The reason for the schism is now unclear, but has been explained by anthropologists as an innate yearning for belonging within the anonymity of the modern metropolis. In contemporary times, the two tribes coexist and interact with little hostility, but old distinctions endure despite the 214 bridges that connect the river's two banks. There is, however, a 215th bridge that, in contrast to its predecessors, is a transitory connection joining the two halves of the metropolis only between the summer months of June and September, during which a common amnesty is held.

This bridge is not the first time the city has attempted to reclaim space from the river. For centuries, the first bridge, named after the city, was habitable, containing shops, houses and a chapel that cantilevered over the water's edge. Northerners and southerners lived side-by-side, rubbing shoulders with one another along a bustling thoroughfare. The bulwarks around the piers of this bridge were so frequent and substantial that they slowed the flow of the river, allowing the water to freeze and the great frost fairs to take place during the winter months. The border between north

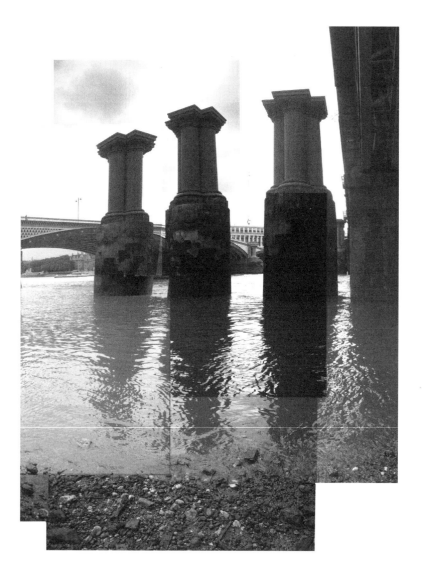

and south would dissolve under a tented city where crowds from the two tribes would gather to race carriages across the ice, play Aqsaqtuk (Inuit football), sup on roast ox, marvel at performing animals and enjoy the thrill rides and sideshows. Having survived burning during the Peasants' Revolt and continual collapse, this grand structure that bridged communities as well as the banks of the river was replaced with a sleekly functional bridge sadly devoid of presence or poetry. Thus the Great River, once brimming with mercantile barges and pontoons on which pageants were held and dramas enacted, is now a lifeless void, redolent of the River Styx over which Charon ferries the dead. The ornate ghost columns of a former railway bridge next to the city's historical centre did little to dispel this impression – four vestigial clusters of massive iron pillars with foliated capitals projected purposelessly from the water, enduring only because of the difficulties presented by their demolition. It is these supports that have been appropriated as the foundations of the Summer Bridge.

The majority of the Summer Bridge is occupied by a beach on which housing, in the form of beach huts, jockeys for position with deckchairs and sandcastles. The huts, decorated in gloss primary colours, contain sleeping and washing facilities for two that satisfy the requirements of shelter and modesty from the beach, effectively

The Summer Bridge is occupied by a beach on which beach huts jockey for position with deckchairs and

sandcastles.

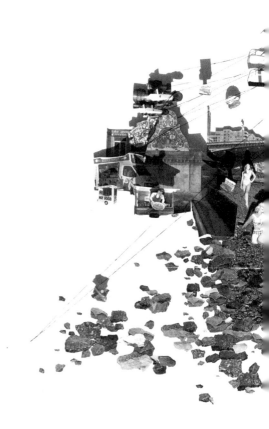

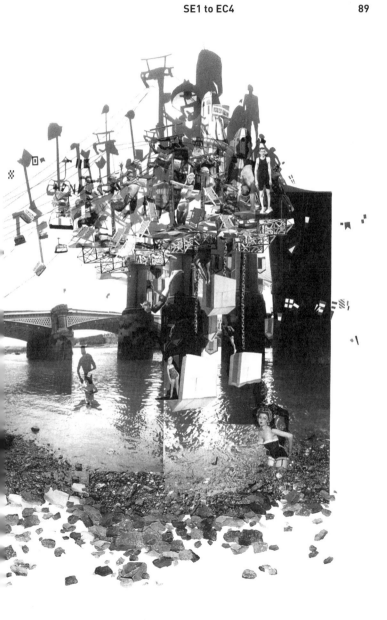

an open-air living room. Periodically, when the weather is fair, the huts are inverted and dipped into the river to collect water for bathing. In contrast to its urban surroundings that are stratified by social mores, the democratic nature of the beach is unmistakable. Sun, sand and sea – the first fickle, the second imported and the last several counties distant – treat the bridge's inhabitants with equal favour, whether prince or pauper, native or tourist, infant or elder.

The bridge is also host to the Summer Fair, replete with merry-go-rounds and helter-skelters, harking back to the spirit of its winter counterpart. With it arrives an unexpected air of abandon and delight, infecting the city's sober straitjacket of propriety. A common pastime involves the launching of projectiles at coconuts, half of which are painted with horned helmets to represent those from the north, the other half depicted in monks' habits representing those from the south. At each end of the bridge are seafood and hamburger stalls from which breakfast, lunch and dinner are prepared and cabled across the length of the beach structure.

Like in a dream, the rules of time are malleable on the Summer Bridge. As a lazy holiday idyll descends a stone's throw away from the frenetic life of the city's business and financial centre, the seaside trappings of Victoriana fuse with 21st Century mindsets and nostalgic childhood memories merge with adult sensibilities. Temporal patterns, along with ritualistic partisanship, are ruthlessly disrupted.

As the nights draw in and families return to work and school, the decks between the abutments and the first and last set of piers are removed, isolating the beach from the banks of the river and leaving a frozen piece of summer, waiting for the sun to catch up with it again. Northerners return to the north and southerners to the south, although crossings become more frequent with each passing year.

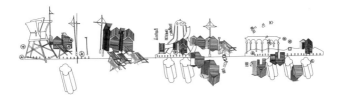

The bridge is also host to the Summer Fair, replete with merry-go-rounds and helter-skelters.

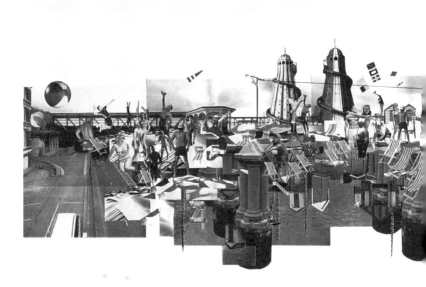

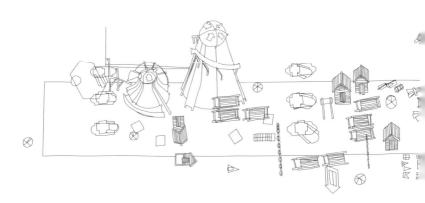

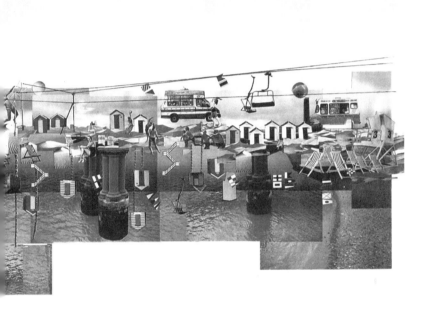

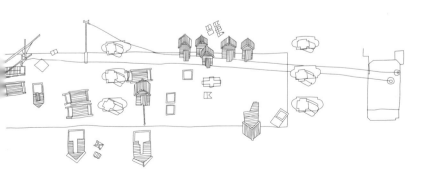

Periodically, when the weather is fair, the huts are inverted and dipped into the river to collect water for bathing.

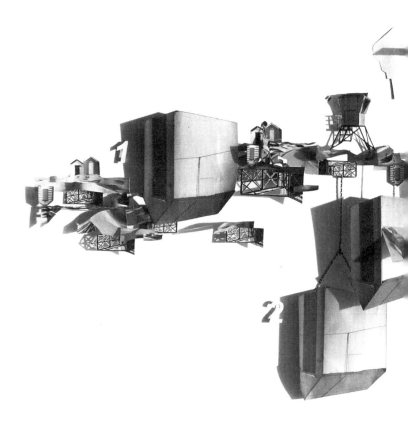

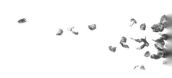

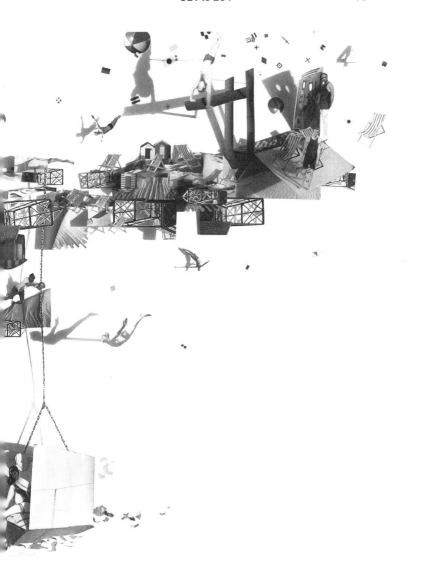

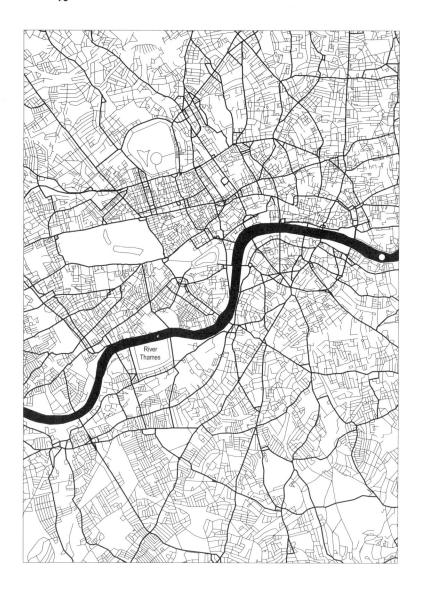

River
Thames

S E 1 6
Darwin's Islands

Darwin's Islands

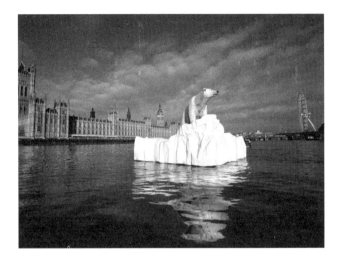

The old magic did not disappear at once but withdrew gradually from the world. Electric illumination had faded first – the bright beacons that had once lit the territory had long since extinguished, their background hum fizzling with a final flourish of animation before falling silent forever. Then, the networks of metal piping that had provided a seemingly limitless supply of water had been invaded by thirsty plant roots, their output reduced to a trickle and then ceasing entirely, however vigorously the pipes were shaken or the valves turned.

Only in one place did the magic survive. Located in the deepest waters of the territory, the London archipelago was the last stronghold of ancient knowledge, tantalizingly inaccessible over the boundless expanse of water that separated the islands from the territory. Visible only at night, the archipelago manifested as a field of twinkling lights in the distance, like stars but drawn towards the horizon and in a far denser configuration.

Each night, Pan and Oliver would stay up to gaze at the fallen stars, giving them names and speculating on their purpose. They regaled each other with children's stories that had been passed down from the elders, embellishing them with new and ever more fanciful details. New London had once been very different – cold and inhospitable, the territory had been many times larger in size, with barely any vegetation. Where concrete and steel had now hybridized with plant life to create an agreeable living environment, there had been hard lifeless surfaces that did not yield underfoot, and barren cage-like enclosures from which air and water was excluded, no doubt places where deviants had been isolated from the remainder of society.

Pan's people had unearthed many unusual implements, plainly originating from an entirely alien belief system. A few of the objects were useful – sharp cutting tools, pieces of twine to bind things together or wheels to transport things one could not easily carry.

The archipelago was the last stronghold of ancient knowledge, inaccessible over the water that separated the islands from the territory.

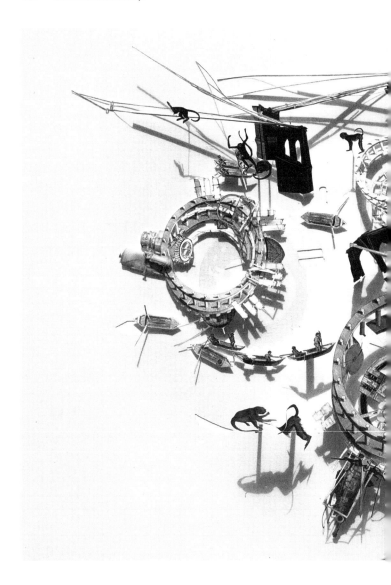

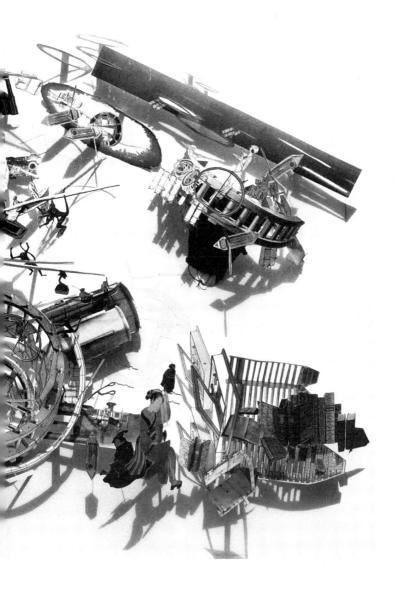

Pan thought he could see monkeys clambering over great steel coracles that were connected together by a network of ropeways.

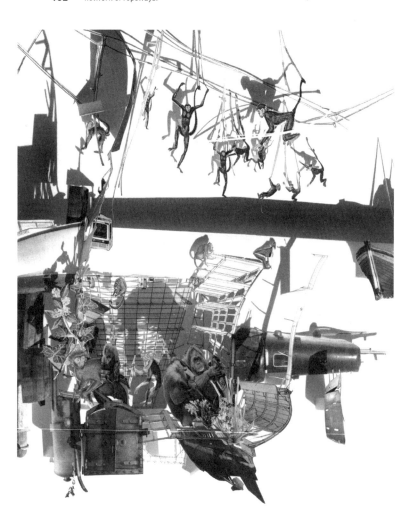

These, the people squabbled and fought over although the spoils were often promptly relinquished for fear of envious reprisal. Far more plentiful, however, were the objects for which function and form were not obviously linked; some would no doubt unearth hidden uses, but the sheer volume and variety of objects indicated the astonishing capacity of Pan's predecessors for extravagance and meaningless diversion.

Pan was unusual in that his interests lay in the spaces that had been inhabited by the ones who had come before, whether they had been deities or extraterrestrials. He was fascinated by the notion of treading in their footsteps and wondered what great calamity could have caused their departure. Together with Oliver, he had discovered vast underground caverns and spaces that would miraculously remain cool when the sun was ascendant, and warm when it retreated from the earth. Another time, the two companions had come across a proliferation of rare flora arranged in complex patterns under which they had found a network of pipes that mirrored the arrangement of flowers above.

Pan's life would change irrevocably the day the great storm ravaged the territory. Several weeks after the confusion and chaos, Pan and Oliver descended to the waterfront to view the stars. The night was

He woke on a dais in the centre of a
large cylindrical gallery. Books lined
the circumference from floor to ceiling.
The ceiling was a long way away.

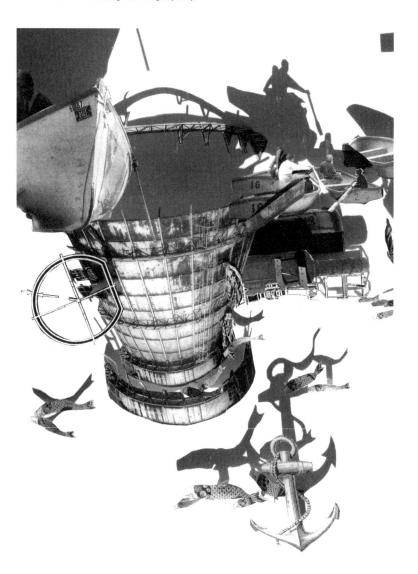

not particularly clear, but the lights of the archipelago burned far brighter than they had in the past. It dawned on Pan that the winds had shifted the islands closer to the territory. They were still distant, but now possibly within reach.

'Pan,' said Oliver, quietly. 'What do you say we take a look? Now, while we still have the chance.' Pan glanced at Oliver, a thousand reasons for dismissing the suggestion as the harebrained whimsy typical of his friend. Then, he gave Oliver a wide grin, grabbed his hand and ran towards the flotsam piled up against the shore. They collected one of the large metal concave discs that usually decorated the crests of buildings, loaded it with hastily gathered jackfruit, bananas and a pail of fresh water, and launched their unlikely seafaring vessel into the waves.

They travelled at night, using the lights from the archipelago to navigate. By day, they rested, hoping they would not drift too far off course without a bearing. The first time Pan drifted off to sleep, Oliver got to his feet, balancing precariously on the disc and shifting his centre of gravity with his arms to counter the motion of the waves. His euphoria and sense of balance did not last long. The disc tipped, Oliver flailed, Pan snorted awake and together they toppled helplessly into the deep. It took them an eternity to clamber back

The inscription read: 'Welcome to Darwin's Islands. Here lies the repository of knowledge and endeavour of homo sapiens, the wise man.'

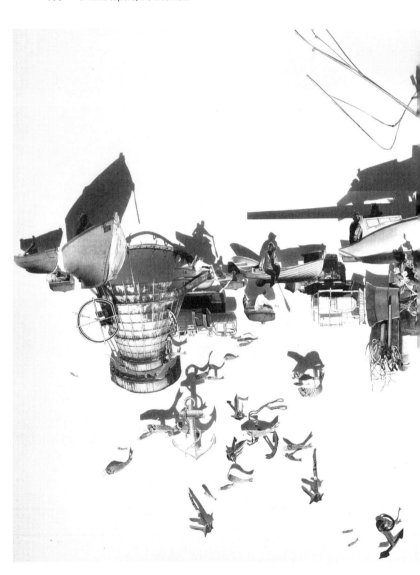

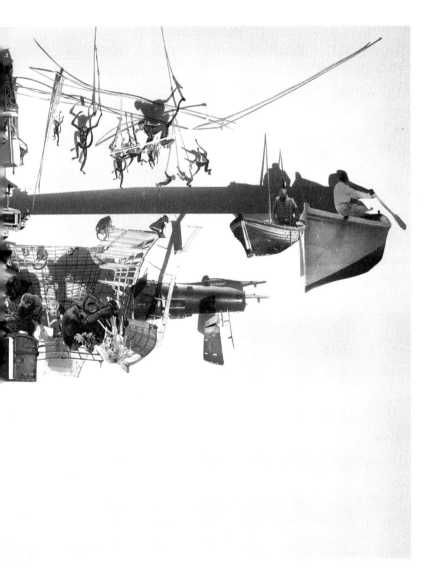

aboard and a reproachful silence reigned until dusk. For all his japes and tomfoolery, however, Pan was immensely grateful to have Oliver as a companion. Without his happy-go-lucky temperament and prodigiously built upper body to help propel them forwards, Pan would have abandoned their quest long ago.

On the fourth day, they could no longer see the mainland and Pan began to panic. Their supply of fresh water was almost depleted and he had never felt so sick in his life. Unbeknownst to Pan, Oliver had already been doctoring his own share of precious fluid with seawater. He could feel tingling within his limbs and his vision was dimming.

'Maybe we should turn back, Oliver.' Pan's companion did not reply but lifted his arm, pointing into the distance. Through a cloud of mist and water vapour was the vague outline of a landmass – the archipelago. They could make out arrays of rotating blades mounted on each island. Oliver, his throat parched and voice weak, opined that they represented a final defence against intruders. Pan was convinced they somehow kept the islands afloat and powered the starlight but was too exhausted to argue.

On the sixth day, dehydrated beyond repair, Oliver's body was no longer capable of sustaining basic bodily functions and succumbed to death's embrace. Pan wailed, weeping bitter tears and cursing the fateful night they determined this course of action. Delirious with grief, he paddled in frenzy toward the spinning blades. As the islands neared, they altered in appearance to reveal their true nature. They were not natural formations but great steel coracles round in form, equal in length and breath, and connected together by a network of ropeways. Like Noah's ark, they were designed not for seafaring, but simply to withstand a deluge. Some were buoyant, others slowly submerging. As the coracles shifted, the ropeways would tangle and untangle. Pan, only half conscious, thought he could see monkeys clambering over them.

On the seventh day, Pan's craft came to rest, colliding with one of the gargantuan structures. He could scull no more. His eyes closed as he felt his body being lifted to safety. He woke on a dais in the centre of a large cylindrical gallery. Books lined the circumference from floor to ceiling. The ceiling was a long way away.

Engraved in the steel floor was an inscription that Pan did not understand. It read: 'Welcome to Darwin's Islands. Here lies the repository of knowledge and endeavour of homo sapiens, the wise man.' Next to it was a painted wooden board with the likeness of ten of Pan's people standing in a row and carrying placards around their necks. They said, 'Laugh now, but one day we'll be in charge.'

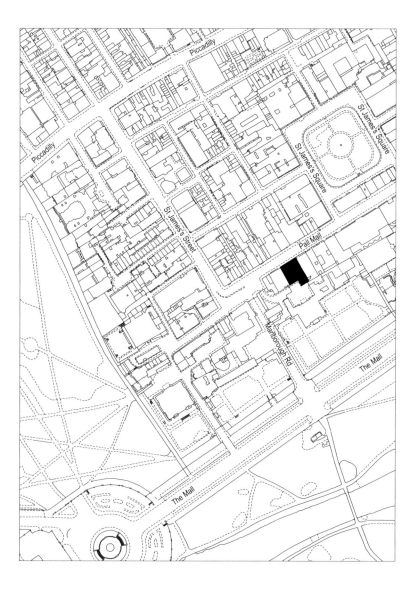

S W 1
Madam Delia's Urban Roost

Madam Delia's Urban Roost

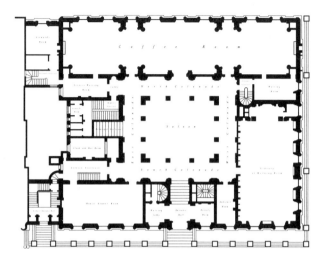

He repaired at once to the dining-room, the nine windows of which open upon a tasteful garden, where the trees were already gilded with an autumn colouring; and took his place at the habitual table, the cover of which had already been laid for him. His breakfast consisted of a side-dish, a broiled fish with Reading sauce, a scarlet slice of roast beef garnished with mushrooms, a rhubarb and gooseberry tart, and a morsel of Cheshire cheese, the whole being washed down with several cups of tea, for which the Reform is famous. He rose at thirteen minutes to one, and directed his steps towards the large hall, a sumptuous apartment adorned with lavishly-framed paintings. A flunkey handed him an uncut

Times, which he proceeded to cut with a skill which betrayed familiarity with this delicate operation.

- 'Around the World in Eighty Days', Jules Verne, 1873

There was once a domestic goddess who lived in a case,
Greeting her gents with full-hearted grace.
She lived with her hens and cows from Devon,
In order to fashion for her guests an urban heaven!

Christopher Watt is brimming with excitement. Due to a confluence of fortuitous circumstances, he is moments away from acquiring the status of 'gentleman'. Enfranchised to vote following the Reform Act of 1885, Christopher is on the cusp of taking over the family concern from his ailing father and has channelled his new-found wealth into smoothing the way into a gentleman's club. The Club in question is 'The Roost', an exclusive if enigmatic establishment in Pall Mall. Admittedly, it is not the Reform Club, the Athenaeum, Boodle's or White's, and although there is a small vain part of Christopher that imagines himself rubbing shoulders with the aristocracy at those august institutions, he decries their members as haughty pompous idlers when he is in the company of his wife and peers. 'Why,' he

The Roost is the smallest building in Pall Mall by some considerable margin, located at No. 79 near the old

Royal Academy building.

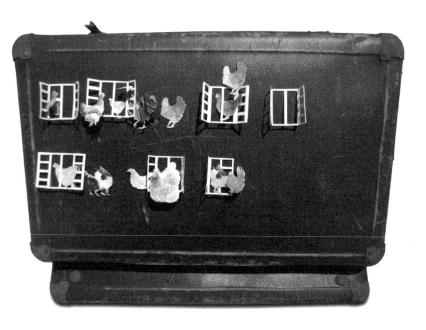

would ask, 'would I wish to spend my leisure time in the company of titled wastrels?'

The final piece of Christopher Watt's elevation to privileged society falls into place with the fall from grace of one of the fifteen Roosters, for such are their members known, leaving an opening for a new affiliate. For Christopher, the Club represents a second home where he will be able to enjoy the singular comforts of male companionship and camaraderie. Just as significantly, it represents a refuge from the neuroses and imprecations of Mrs Watt, his long-suffering wife of seventeen years. Had he been alive, that pompous ass Samuel Johnson would have declared him the most unclubbable of men, being the heir to a roadside manure clearing business, yet here he is, about to be welcomed into the most talked about club in the whole of the city.

The Roost is the smallest building in Pall Mall by some considerable margin, located at No. 79 near the old Royal Academy building and the only property on the south side of the street not owned by the Crown. Where the established clubs have commissioned the leading architects of the day such as Barry, Wilkins and Smirke to replicate the palatial splendour of foreign lands, the Roost's design is a technological marvel and unashamedly British. The founders

The leather bound façade of the house is a living screen of cooing hens arranged on the building's windowsills.

116

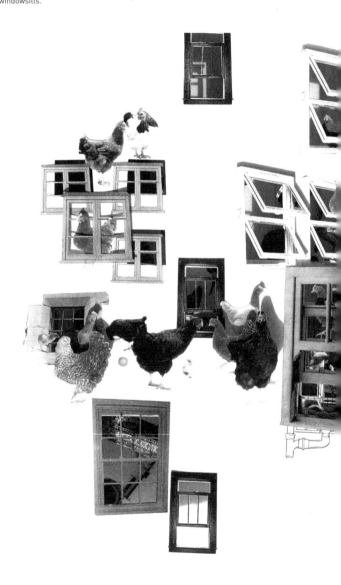

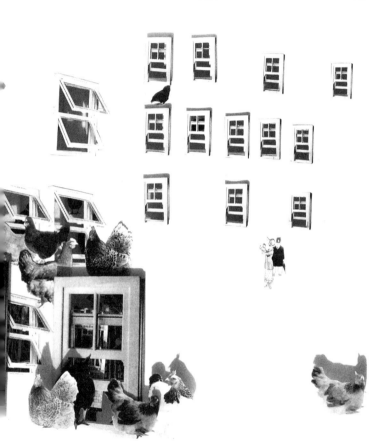

The habitable spaces within extend and unfold each morning to provide a stage set for grooming, relaxation and formal dining.

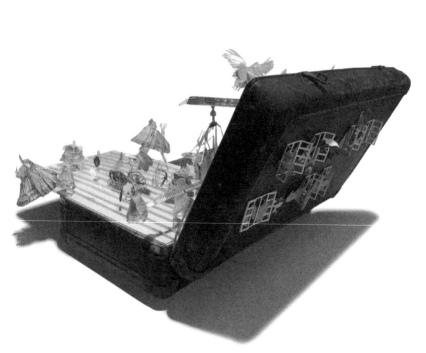

of the Roost have sensibly eschewed the vulgar Italianate stylings of the Reform Club or Royal Automobile Club and elected to draw up plans themselves with the assistance of Thomas Robinson, an artist and inventor who will later become the inspiration for Norman Hunter's Professor Theophilus Branestawm.

The structure itself is a large vintage briefcase, a form perhaps symbolic of home comforts away from home, perhaps simply a cock of the snook at the Travellers' Club. In stark contrast to the respectable features and proportions of its neighbours, the leather bound façade of the house is a living screen of cooing hens arranged on the building's windowsills. The preened feathers of the birds animate and add colour to the façade, disturbed occasionally by feral cats that temporarily shatter this veil of bucolic serenity. Behind this façade, formality is discarded and replaced by theatre. The habitable spaces within extend and unfold each morning to provide a stage set for grooming, relaxation and formal dining.

And so with closed collar, jacket and tie, Christopher skips gaily up the steps of the Roost Club, raps on the door with his cane and is greeted by a smiling middle-aged lady in a pinafore. Madam Delia is her name, the hostess and orchestrator of the Club's day-to-day activities. Her welcome is effusive, a world away from the cold

The bathrooms are arranged with oriental screens, patterned rugs and portraits of reactionary gentlemen.

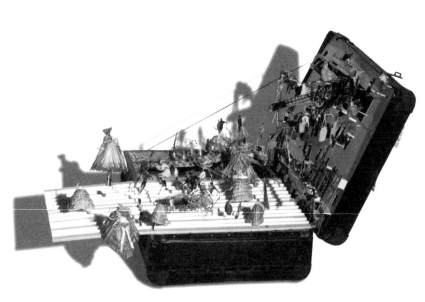

disdain of Christopher's butler at the Watt household.

This being Christopher's first visit to the Club, he must undergo a rite of initiation. He is mildly titillated as he is shown into a changing room constructed from crinoline petticoats, and recalls that everything in the house is feminine other than the gentlemen who frequent it. Christopher is asked to change into football attire. He is then instructed to hurtle down a perfume-sprinkled field of grass, 'the field', and kick an oestrogen-filled ball between two upright poles and above a cross-piece, 'the goal', some ten yards distant. This he does with aplomb, stirring memories of schooldays and the brash audaciousness of youth. A mechanical cock crows and a rope-geared sedan with multiple pulleys hoists the newly crowned Rooster up to the floor above.

In the colonial comfort of the bathrooms, Christopher relaxes in self-congratulation. The bathrooms are arranged with oriental screens, patterned rugs and portraits of the reactionary gentlemen who have paved the way to the Roost Club's establishment, such as Gladstone, Palmerston and Disraeli. There is no roof to the bathrooms, and being midwinter, the only light comes from chandeliers in the shape of chickens that dangle from a crane. After a luxurious shower with state-of-the-art pumped hot water,

The eggs were laid by Leghorn hens within buckets lit from beneath with Swan carbon-fibre light bulbs to regulate their hatching cycles.

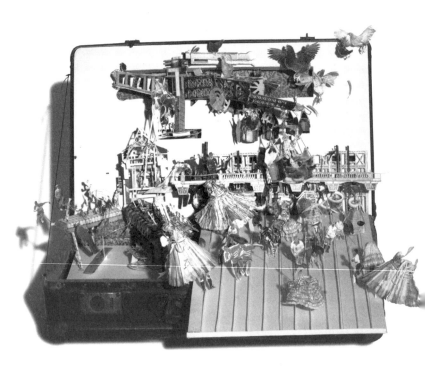

Christopher returns to his chair where he is given a shave. The facing wall, a curtain of newspapers and periodicals, scrolls almost imperceptibly across his field of vision, allowing him to pick up news stories and what appear to be current affairs. Christopher notes, however, that many of the papers are dated and yellowing.

Clean-shaven and pampered, the chair conveys Christopher to a candlelit dinner table suspended above Madam Delia's kitchen. Already present are the other members of the Roost, groomed and be-suited in their best attire to welcome their new confrère. Each in turn welcomes Christopher with a 'Hail fellow, well met!' although Christopher is mildly dismayed that they do not get to their feet to greet him. Before he can ponder the ruddy complexions and bloated paunches of his newfound comrades, he is distracted by the sumptuous breakfast laid out before him. Most of the spread consists of eggs and cream, prepared in a host of different ways for which Madam Delia has rightfully claimed the title 'doyenne of culinary hospitality'. The eggs, he is told, were laid a few hours ago by Leghorn hens within buckets lit from beneath with Swan carbon-fibre light bulbs to regulate their hatching cycles; the cream comes from a Devonshire cow which resides in a stall next to the oestrogen-watered rugby field on which it grazes. Christopher watches in astonishment as Madam Delia attaches pumps to the

The Roost's reputation for lavish comfort grows while its members within endure a miserable self-inflicted captivity.

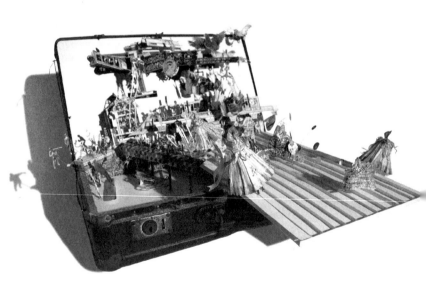

cow's udders and hoists it to the level of the table. The Roosters press their glasses to a knot of dangling tubes, anticipating the delivery of the very finest, fattest milk as the suspended cow begins to lactate.

No business or trade conversation is permitted, a stipulation that Christopher is immensely grateful for. Moreover, one does not speak of family affairs – the Club is after all a haven from wives and children. The Roosters are thus bound in wretched silence, daring one another to mention the unpleasant farmyard smell or the piles that have developed on their posteriors from prolonged sitting. Non-attendance by the Roosters, however, is unthinkable, entailing the humiliation of explaining to their wives why they are at home when they have lavished their fortunes on their vain enterprise. Outside the Club then, the Roost's reputation for lavish comfort grows while its members within endure a miserable self-inflicted captivity.

A cowpat drops onto the floor. The fifteen Roosters feign ignorance, pondering on the irony that this celebrated institution, designed to cosset the male ego, is in fact responsible for its emasculation. Christopher is reminded of Conan Doyle's Diogenes Club in which no member is allowed to acknowledge the existence of another on pain of expulsion, convinced that the young author's similar

This celebrated institution, designed to cosset the male ego, is in fact responsible for its emasculation.

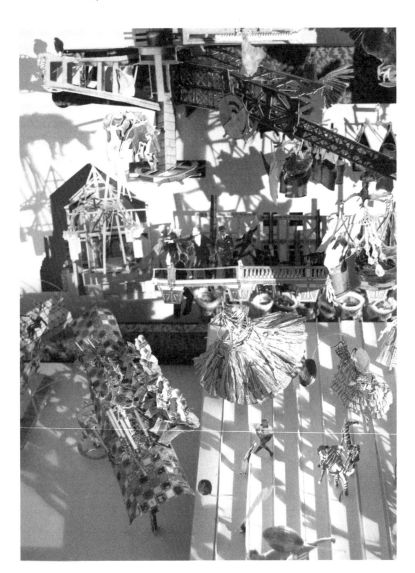

experiences at other clubs had prompted its creation.

The breakfast is so cloyingly rich that Christopher wonders how long it will be before he becomes obese and sedentary like the other fourteen men at the table, how long before his virility will be irreparably impaired by fat and female hormones. He eats steadily with his silver spoon and feigned enthusiasm. He has already become one of the club.

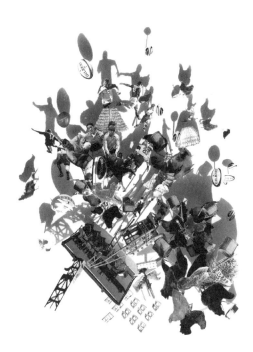

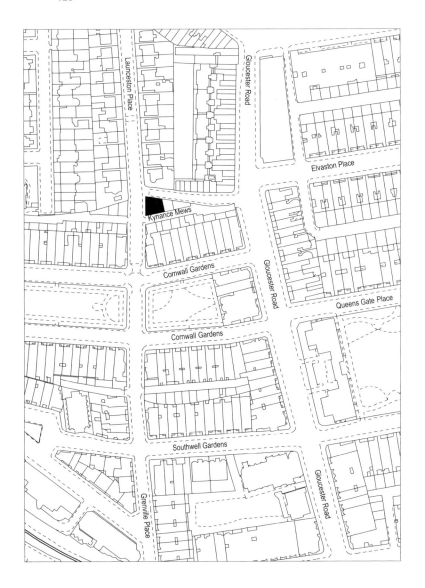

S W 7

Carousel

Carousel

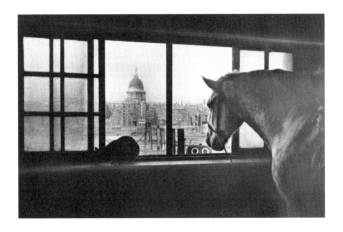

Horsey horsey don't you stop
Just let your feet go clippetty clop
The tail goes swish and the wheels go round
Giddy up, we're homeward bound.

- Traditional nursery rhyme, Roberts, Box, Cox and Butler, 1938

The siren wailed. William grimaced, nudged his horse towards the side of the road and pressed the brake key on his Blackberry until his mount came to a standstill. A traffic policeman cantered up beside him and swung out of his saddle in a single fluid motion.

'Morning, Sir,' he said in a singsong voice William considered to be excessively cheerful. 'Please dismount.' William placed both hands on the pommel of his motorized saddle, eased himself up in his stirrups and slid down to the ground.

'I've stopped you for reckless riding. Are you aware of the speed you were travelling at, Sir?'

'Um. A little faster than I should have been, I suppose. I'm running late for a very important meeting.' William, correctly anticipating the warden's expression that sublimated seamlessly from false cheeriness to frosty reproval, quickly added, 'Although I know that's no excuse.' Inwardly, William groaned at his stupidity for speeding within spitting distance of the old Remount Depot where the mounted police had re-established their headquarters.

'Indeed, Sir. There is no excuse for maltreating your horse. You were travelling at 11 miles per hour. Do you have any idea how many pedestrians have been killed by speeding in the past year? I will exercise my discretion this time and not caution you under the Horse Welfare Act but I am going to issue you with an on-the-spot fine.'

William was swept along in a wave of brilliant colour, decorative livery, ornate coats of arms, blaring horns and the syncopated clatter of hooves.

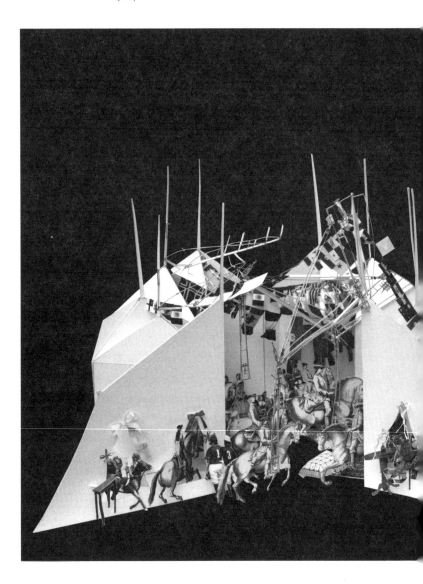

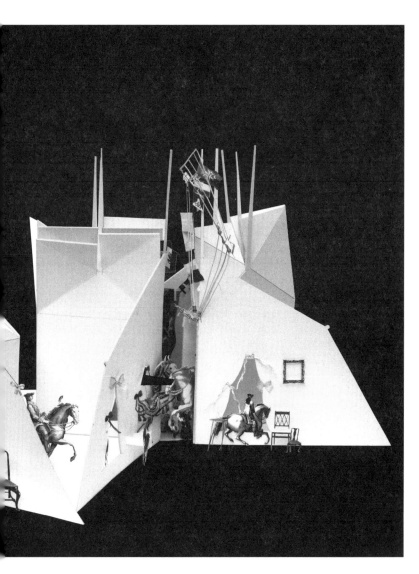

William encountered the same people every day – not only his family and work colleagues – but the familiar faces he chanced upon riding along the road.

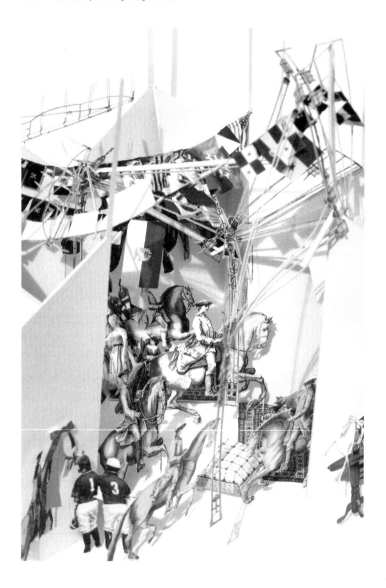

William traded in his details for a penalty notice that he snapped into his briefcase before climbing back onto the nut-brown mare. Horse maltreatment? What a crock! His pampered horse could do with the exercise; with the mobility assistance saddle, it barely broke a sweat.

Having failed his riding test several times, William disliked travelling by horse, even without the vexation of officious wardens, and had refused to relinquish his SUV until the very day the Equine Transport act had come into force. Railing against his existence as part of an unholy chimera of man, beast and mechanical contraption, William wistfully recalled the comforts of suspension, automatic climate control and manure-free air, although admittedly, he crossed the city no slower on horseback than he had by motorcar. At the time of the changeover, there had been endless controversy over the banishment of motorcars and their replacement with equestrian transport – each horse, the protestors claimed, would consume the farming produce from five acres of land annually, enough to feed eight people. The problems of manure, methane generation and vermin infestations had also been raised, but Mayor Johnson had managed to force the act through. The solution had been elegant and effective – to prevent the banks of storey-high dung that had ground Victorian London to a stinking halt, manure was collected in

William turned off the Gloucester Road and the cacophony faded into the staccato canter of a single horse.

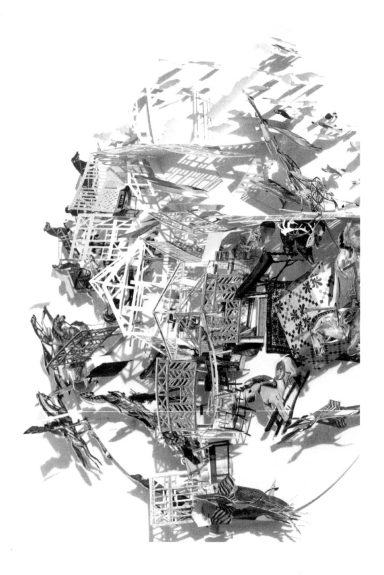

hoppers mounted under the horses and channeled into miniaturized anaerobic digesters. The methane generated would then be used to power biogas engines, thereby reducing the burden on the mounts. William was struck by the irony that the automobile, hailed as an environmental saviour in the last century, had been replaced by the very problem it had usurped using the same specious logic.

William was not by nature a duplicitous man, but his absence at the meeting he was supposedly rushing to attend would probably go unnoticed – a tiresome committee meeting where everyone would clamour to be heard and nothing would be agreed. Instead of making his way to the insurance company where he worked as an actuary then, William stopped off at the Kensington and Chelsea Town Hall on the King's Road to discharge his fine.

'How are you today Mr Watt? Another speeding fine?' asked the police clerk at the penalty gaily. It was more a statement than a question. William looked sheepish. 'Afraid so, Constable Withers. Mrs Watt is going to be apoplectic.'

'Sorry to hear that Mr W. The wardens can be a little overzealous at times, what with the quotas they try to meet. I should think you'd be entitled to a bulk discount by now though.'

William groaned at his stupidity for speeding near the old Remount Depot where the mounted police had re-established their headquarters.

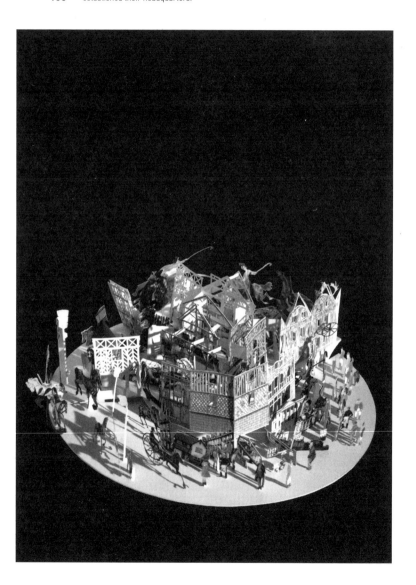

'If only,' said William ruefully. 'Oh, and I have another incidence of tack theft to report. A bridle. That's the reason I was running late and speeding in the first place.'

'My word, Mr Watt! That's the third theft you've reported this week and it's what, Wednesday? I'll just get you the pro forma,' said the clerk, licking his thumb and picking up a sheaf of multi-coloured triplicatenforms. 'Did you have the London and Birmingham bars installed on your front door like the crime prevention officer suggested?'

'Yes. Yes we have, but it won't be any use. There are no signs of break-in whatsoever. We have no idea how the thieves get in, it's like a locked room mystery from a crime novel. I don't suppose you've had any luck with tracking down the halter and stirrups that were stolen last week? I went to some trouble ordering particularly garish livery and also got everything laser marked.'

'Afraid laser marking isn't much help unless the stolen goods are recovered, Mr Watt. Maybe you ought to think about tagging your equipment with RFIDs.'

'RFI what?'

William fetched his horse from the office valet and joined Chelsea's throng of mounted commuters, omnibuses and hansoms.

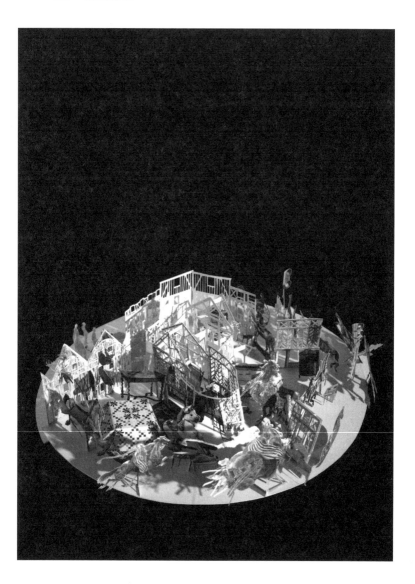

'RFID, Radio Frequency Identification. They're little chips that you can attach to your equipment that can be traced with a GPS.'

'Hmm. Sounds like something worth investigating.' William completed the forms and handed them to back to Constable Withers who cast a brief eye over them, nodding his head.

'That all looks in order. We'll send you a receipt by email. Let's hope we don't see you again this week, Mr Watt.' William bade the clerk a good day and went to collect his horse from the underground car park off Sloane Square. Like most people, William still called them car parks, and the only real change to the infrastructure had been shallower ramps and the installation of tethering posts. If car engines could be measured in units of horse power, why could horses not be kept in car parks?

It struck William that he encountered the same people every day – not only his family, work colleagues and individuals like Constable Withers, but the familiar faces he chanced upon riding along the road, at the canteen or down the pub that he had never engaged in conversation, never negotiated the line that divided stranger from acquaintance. Collectively, they formed an involuntary community of urban strangers, bound together through the city's daily pattern and personal routines. The same sequence of events, over and over again. There were subtle differences, of course, but there were days when William could picture himself as an ant on a Moebius loop in an Escher drawing.

At one o'clock William ate the lunch his wife had packed, scanned the obituary page of the 'Financial Times' as was his custom, ordered a new bridle to be delivered the same day, and shuffled some paperwork for the remainder of the day before setting off for home. Fetching his horse from the office valet, he joined Chelsea's throng of mounted commuters, omnibuses and hansoms. Curiously, the return to equine transport had re-established a long-forgotten lexicon of vehicles – cabs were once again cabriolets, buses omnibuses, trucks truckles, and vans caravans. Despite himself, William was swept along in a wave of brilliant colour, decorative livery, ornate coats of arms, blaring horns and the syncopated clatter of hooves euphemistically known outside the borough as the Chelsea symphony.

As William turned off Gloucester Road, the cacophony faded into the staccato canter of a single horse, modulating in timbre as the road surface changed from macadam to granite setts. William dismounted and led the mare through the stone arch of Kynance

Mews, past the birch tree, honeysuckle and hydrangeas towards the mews house he had renovated three years ago to house the horse and its requisite equestrian paraphernalia. The house and its curtilage were grade listed, a place in which horses and humans could feign residence within semi-bucolic surroundings and in stark contrast to the pastiche urban stables that had proliferated in the area. William unlocked the heavy timber door and guided the mare under the stained timber bressumer beam into a room whose function had changed from stable to garage and back again. His daughter, Cassandra, came rushing in to greet him. Cassie, the apple of his eye, the centre around which his world revolved. Lifting her into the air, he twirled her around several times until he began to feel dizzy, whereupon he lowered her gently to the ground.

'Can I pet her, Daddy? Please?' asked Cassandra.

'Just for a while, then, darling. And only her neck, back or withers, not her head or flanks, or she'll get nervous. Billy will be along to groom her properly in half-an-hour or so,' said William, detaching the powered saddle from the mare and rolling it to the corner of the room.

'Can she stay at home tomorrow so I can ride her after school?'

William heard the police siren signalling that it was time for him to pay the fare for another ride on life's merry-go-round.

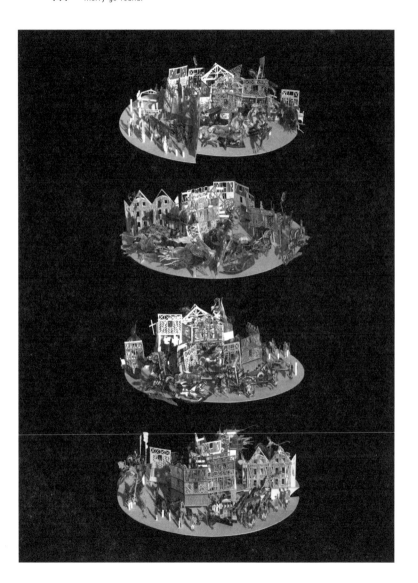

'Not tomorrow dear. But sometime soon, I promise.'

The next morning, William was running late again. He had taken the turnout rug off his horse only to discover that the stirrups were missing. He set off for work swearing sulphurously and gripping the sides of the horse uncertainly with his legs. Cassandra, meanwhile, was sadly looking at the growing collection of bridles, harnesses, reins, bits and halters under her bed. William was half way along the Fulham Road before he heard the police siren signalling that it was time for him to pay the fare for another ride on life's merry-go-round.

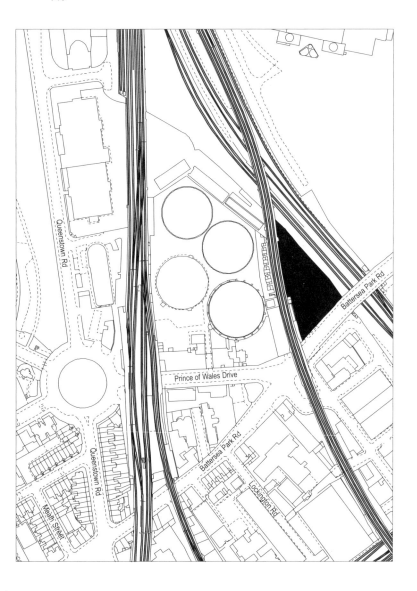

S W 1 1

Battersea Dating Agency

Battersea Dating Agency

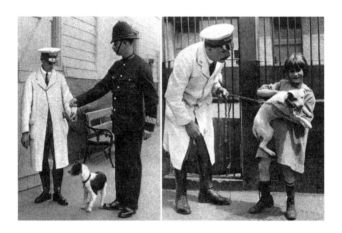

I am his Highness' dog at Kew; Pray tell me sir, whose dog are you?

- Frederick Louis, Prince of Wales (1707–51)

Jane Goodall is an ethnocynologist and director of the New Battersea Centre for Dogs. She has overseen the transformation of this venerable institution into a thriving business. Curtis Jones speaks to her.

CJ: Most people are probably unfamiliar with the term

ethnocynologist. Perhaps you can start by explaining what you do.

JG: Yes, I often get met with blank looks when I introduce myself. Ethnocynology is the study of dogs, particularly in their cultural contexts and their relationship with man. The domestic dog has had a key role in shaping human civilization over the millennia and in turn has been shaped by humans to have specific characteristics, either through training or breeding. We have selected desirable traits and characters and recombined them as if we were piecing together a collage into something new that is sometimes a fruitful intermarriage, sometimes an abomination. Even more remarkably, we have managed to subjugate a species to the extent that it willingly denies its natural instincts – chasing other animals, urinating, barking, and digging holes, intercourse – in deference to human preferences. Dogs live by our rules rather than their own. In this light, the domestic dog becomes virtually a human creation, or perhaps recreation – our Frankenstein's monster, for want of a better description. Despite this, the species has been little studied in the anthropological terms that it surely warrants.

CJ: Claude Lévi-Strauss once said that animals were 'bons à penser'. He mentions this in reference to fairy stories in which animals are anthropomorphized, reflecting human characters and

A perfect opportunity to transform a
beautiful but underutilized structure
from our industrial heritage into a
150   terrific piece of spatial theatre.

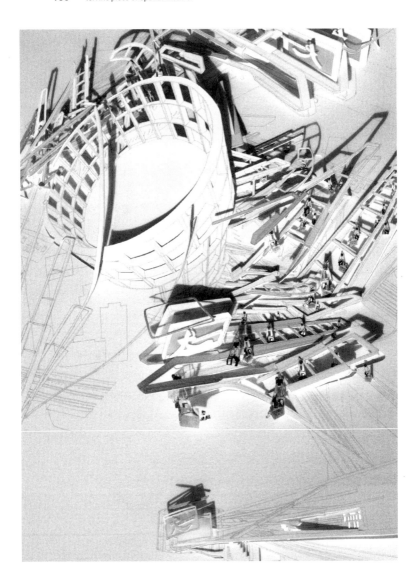

traits to expose human responses. Perhaps this is no less true of real animals, particularly canines that we have such a strong emotional bond with?

JG: Yes, dogs tell us a lot about ourselves. Lévi-Strauss goes as far as to call dogs metonymical humans. It's unfortunate that familiarity obscures the extraordinary relationship between dogs and man. Bryan Cummins, the anthropologist who coined the term ethnocynology, comments that the dog is 'neither fully of culture or nature'. He explains that different human societies have shaped the dog into precisely whatever roles people might have for the dog.

CJ: The Centre is also a venue for dog racing. How did this come about?

JG: Well, we took over the Nine Elms Gas Works from the Royal Mail who were using it for storage and a sorting depot. As you might have noticed, the gas works are circular in shape. Two circuits of the circumference make 525 yards, the standard length for a dog race. I say this flippantly, but this presented us with a perfect opportunity to transform a beautiful but underutilized structure from our industrial heritage into a terrific piece of spatial theatre. The races obviously differ from those on a conventional track as the dogs are

The gas works are circular in shape –
two circuits of the circumference make
525 yards, the standard length for a
dog race.

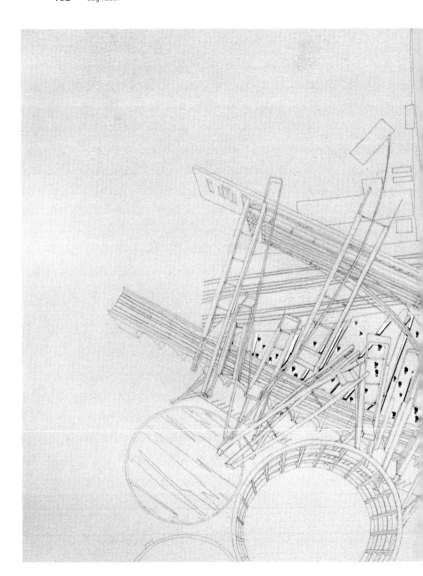

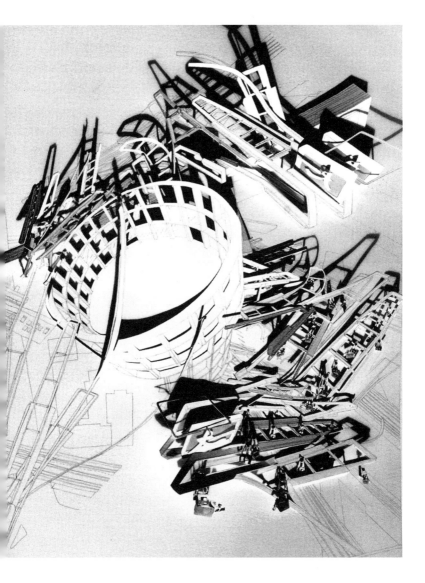

The spectators sit on benches in the centre of the arena and watch the dogs race around them in a reversal of the usual arrangement.

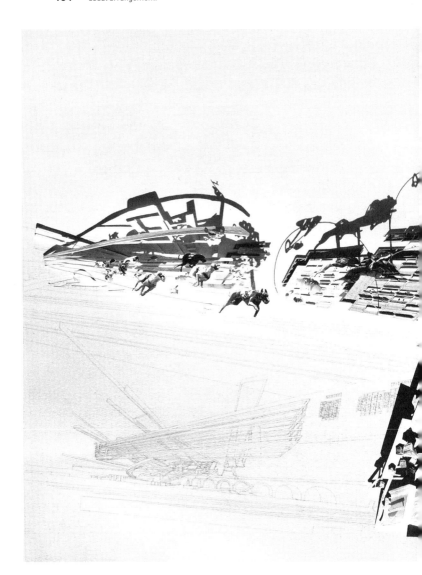

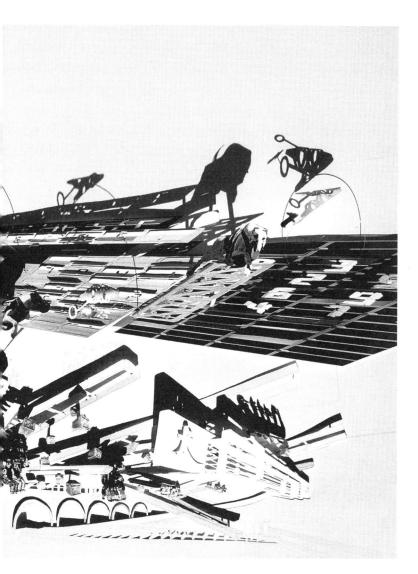

The dogs are positioned vertically one above the other in an inhabitable billboard, which enhances the spectacle for the punter.

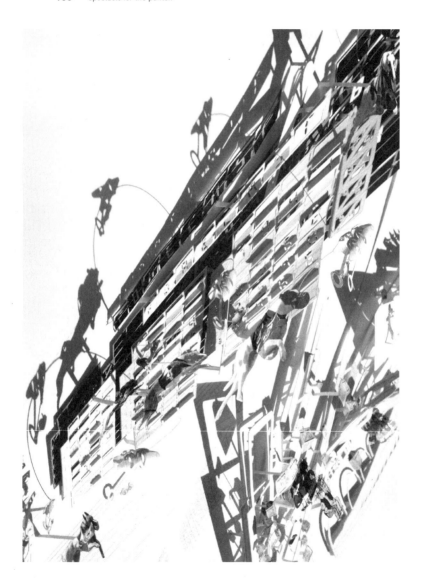

positioned vertically one above the other in an inhabitable billboard, which enhances the spectacle for the punter. The spectators sit on benches in the centre of the arena and watch the dogs race around them in a reversal of the usual arrangement.

Dog racing, which evolved from the ancient pursuit of coursing, remains one of the country's most popular spectator sports and is just one other example of how dogs have assimilated into our culture. Although there are tracks in Wimbledon, Romford and Crayford, there is a demand for additional venues, especially since the closure of Walthamstow Stadium in 2008. The dog racing at Battersea is undoubtedly one of the more controversial elements of our operation, but here we can ensure that greyhounds are well cared for and monitored by our in-house vets, that there is no doping, and that the dogs are adopted into good homes after their retirement.

CJ: Besides the conversion of the gas tower, the Centre uses space creatively in less obvious ways.

JG: One of the innovations of the Centre is the flexibility of its use and the sharing of facilites. Most race meetings take place in the evening which would leave the arena empty for most of the time.

When dusk falls, arrays of portable recycled-card kennels are lowered to the ground to house the animals.

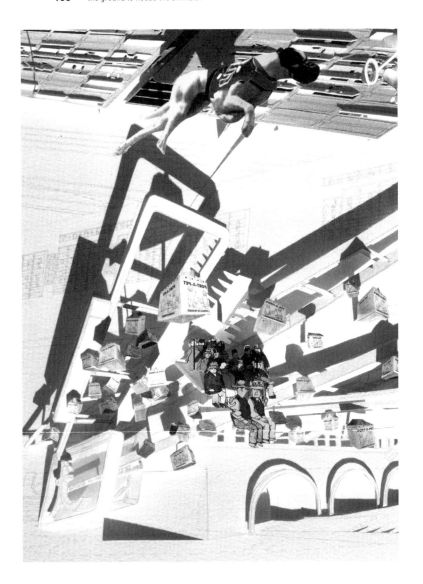

Instead, the grounds operate as a private park during the day, and are used for training purposes or to exercise the dogs. When dusk falls, arrays of portable recycled-card kennels are lowered to the ground to house the animals. The home's primary veterinary services as well as grooming and rehabilitation facilities are located under the park.

CJ: You mention that the decision to hold dog-racing events at Battersea was controversial. Can you expand on that?

JG: My two roles are sometimes difficult to reconcile. When I have my anthropologist hat on, all aspects of the man and dog bond fascinate me, and that includes cruel and unsavoury practices such as dog fighting, baiting and other blood sports. As director of the New Battersea Centre for Dogs, however, my main concern is the welfare of the dogs.

CJ: The city is not a natural habitat for any animal. How does the dog fit into a modern metropolis like London?

JG: Dogs, as most people know, are descended from wolves, although there is also a persuasive argument that they share ancestry with jackals. Neither are naturally suited to the concrete

The Centre is a microcosm of the city –
the training yards, behavioural clinics
and grooming parlours are all named
160   after areas of London.

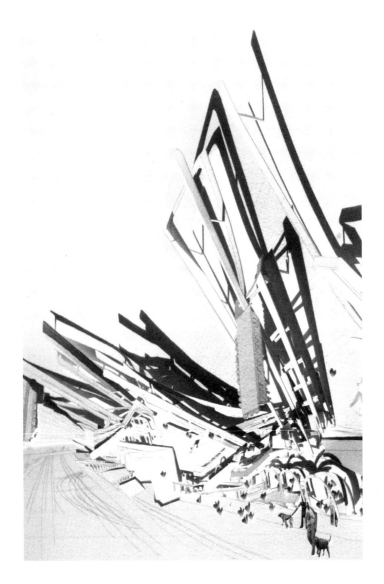

jungle, but London remains the greenest city in Europe, possibly the world; a third of London is green space. Although large dogs should be free to exercise over a large area, most dogs are well adapted to live in the city and have played significant roles in London's history. In early times, dogs would improve urban sanitation by disposing of food scraps and human waste, and other than the self-evident roles that canines have played in hunting and as watchdogs, there have been other more unusual jobs that dogs have performed. Turnspit dogs, for example would turn the spit in 18th and 19th Century kitchens to ensure that the roast cooked evenly. In case there are any readers imagining a dog rotating the spit with its paws, I hate to disappoint you but the dogs would operate the spit from inside a wire barrel like you might find in a hamster cage.

There is a sad tale to tell too, though. During the Great Plague of 1665, the aldermen of the city believed that dogs and cats were responsible for spreading the disease and were eradicated from London in a mass cull which the historian Mark Jenner calls the 'Great Dog Massacre'. All this did, of course, was remove the rat's natural predators from the city, fuelling the contagion. An interesting social aside is that greyhounds, spaniels and hounds of the gentry were excluded from the cull.

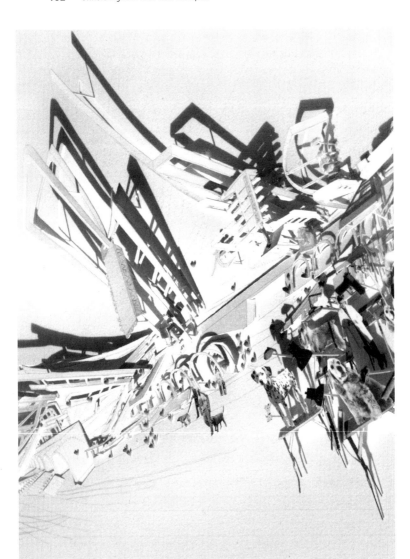

The dog-dating scheme brings prospective
162   owners together with their ideal pet.

CJ: The Centre for Dogs has not always been at Battersea. Originally it was known as the Temporary Home for Lost and Starving Dogs and was housed in a stable in Holloway. What prompted the move?

JG: That happened a long time ago! The home moved to Battersea in 1871. It was originally established by a marvellously eccentric lady called Mary Tealby who grew concerned about the welfare of stray dogs in North London. At the time, the press ridiculed her for inappropriate sentimentalism in the light of the terrible living conditions of the poor. Mary Tealby should be remembered as a pioneer in both bringing animal welfare to the public consciousness and for the social engagement of women. The home was forced to move to Battersea after complaints of noise and nuisance. The Centre at Battersea is now a microcosm of the city – the training yards, behavioural clinics and grooming parlours are all named after areas of London.

CJ: Are pet dogs a relatively recent phenomenon, then?

JG: In England, the concept of the dog as pet only began during the Middle Ages when regulation came into force. In the late 14th Century, it was decreed that dogs would be forbidden to roam the streets of London untethered, which inevitably led to the distinction

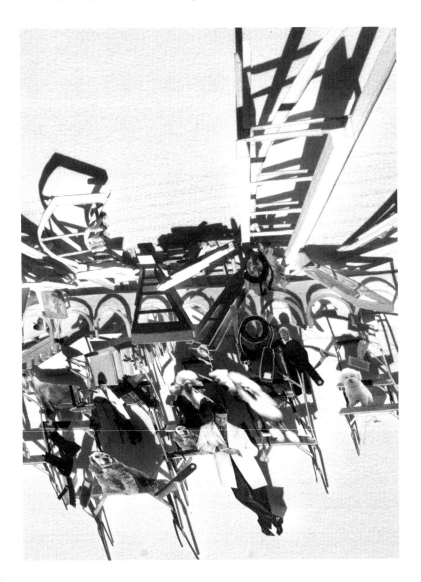

The home's primary veterinary services
as well as grooming and rehabilitation
164 facilities are located under the park.

between household dogs and strays.

Regrettably, the emergence of canines as pets has led to a fundamental change in our relationship with them. The function of the dog today, barring highly specialized animals such as guide dogs and sniffer dogs, has been reduced to that of the accessory. Even lapdogs, said to originate in Himalayan temples to keep Buddhist priests warm, used to fulfill the purpose of keeping the feet of women warm in church.

CJ: From what you have said, the future of the dog as an autonomous species in the light of widespread urbanization looks bleak. What means are there to redress this situation?

JG: One thing that canines still provide is companionship, an aspect that has become all the more important because of the alienation a large city like London engenders. There exists a culture of loneliness and general wariness of strangers. Dogs are natural icebreakers – so much so that there are dating agencies for pet-owners. Perhaps the most radical aspect of the Centre, but also the one that unjustifiably attracts the most ridicule, is the dog-dating scheme which is designed to bring prospective owners together with their ideal pet. While we are not the first institution to introduce dog-dating – there is a pet services agency in France called Gardicanin which matches dogs with host families during the summer break and is modelled on a speed-dating setup – we attempt to expand the criteria for matchmaking to embrace the polytropic nature of the Centre. Specialized training for working animals such as guide and police dogs are now consolidated here at Battersea so we match dogs with the blind, deaf and police. We also provide animal-assisted therapy dogs for medical conditions such as Alzheimer's. The average person does not have these requirements, and potential pets are projected onto advertising screens in the park to see if a match can be made. Of course the owners are vetted too and have to go through an evaluation to obtain their dog license. We do try to engineer new connections between our wards and potential owners to bring a new relevancy to dogs in our society again. If you wanted, for example, to own a greyhound or try your hand at truffle hunting either for your own enjoyment or as a commercial business, we would be able to match you with a suitable companion.

BITCH SEEKING DOG

- Petite brunette, young, very slim seeks good CD male specimen with GSOH.
- Attractive, excitable, no D/D, independent, American Jack

Russell WLTM SBM, 3–4yrs, for LTR. Enjoys long romantic walks, car journeys etc.

- Sophisticated, very attractive, educated Labrador retriever looking to meet attractive, charismatic man for W/S and PNP.

- COCKER SPANIEL, BDSM WLTM IRL TV TS GHM FTM ISO DTE HWP LTR or PNP NSA.

- DESPERATELY SEEKING NORFOLK Terrier. Young excitable Bichon Frisé, 2, looking to meet like-minded bitch for NSA fun.

- (HIT ME) BABY ONE MORE TIME! Bearded Collie adventurous, slimmish, responds well to dominant commands, leather collars and leads essential.

- ORIENTAL, PEKINESE, of a certain age, brown hair, slimmish build WLTM nice, gentle, honest man to treat her like a 'lady'.

- BLACK, ATTRACTIVE BITCH, 6, educated seeks attractive sugar daddy, 40–53, to be wined, dined and spoiled.

- GORGEOUS, FEMININE BITCH Cavalier King Charles Spaniel seeks attractive MOTOS for heavy conversation and warmth.

- SUCCESSFUL BITCH, 3, enjoys sports and the outdoors, WLTM tall outgoing man.

- LEAD THE WAY! Young bitch, dark hair, comfortable with leather collars, BDSM ISO HWP, W/E, TV, NSA. CURIOUS?

- VERY ASSERTIVE, EXPERIENCED, BDSM, ex-military bitch seeks slim, perhaps athletic MOTSS, outwardly feisty but inwardly desiring guidance.

- ADVENTUROUS W/E Great Dane, 87cm, Str8 seeks lady or couple for daytime adult fun. SW.
- SEXY VERY ATTRACTIVE, tall intelligent often, Pre-Op requires mutually rewarding liaisons, travel etc. with very solvent SWM, possible LTR.
- CHEEKY LADY WANTED by attractive tramp, 9, for naughty but nice fun.

MAN SEEKING BITCH

- GENUINE SPRINGER good looks, kind, even funny on occasions, hard working, seeks slim/petite, attractive female, 2–3, for mutual, emotional investment.
- KING SEEKS HIS QUEEN, Cavalier King Spaniel seeks likewise, young male, medium build, seeks a charming bitch, 3–4, for LTR.
- TALL PROFESSIONAL, intelligent Weimaraner, 4,5 grey eyes, seeks mature, glamorous Bichon for fun, friendship and romance.
- AFFECTIONATE, PASSIONATE, GERMAN Shepherd, 3,8, likes socializing, seeks loyal, energetic bitch, 3–4, N/S for RTS.
- GENUINE, TALL, FRIENDLY Alsace, young 3s, likes walks in the park, continental food seeks female with warm personality and

inquisitive nature.

- STOCKY MALE, 5, dark hair seeks white and faun female, over 4, attractive, well-built, loving, caring tactile, trustworthy.
- DOMESTICATED, EDUCATED, PROFESSIONAL Dalmatian, 4 and a half, fit, seeks assured slim female, 2 and a half to 3, who's looking for loyalty, devotion and attention.
- LAST TANGO IN TOOTING BEC, good-looking male, 4.5, friendly, DTE, GSOH, seeks open-minded bitch WLTM IRL.
- DO RIGHT WOMAN, DO RIGHT MAN, DR. FEELGOOD come rescue me! AZN M4M seeks M4MM stocky build chow-chow.

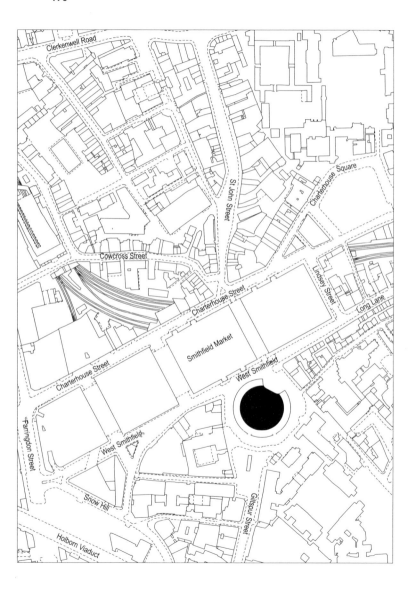

E C 1
The Nocturnal Tower

The Nocturnal Tower

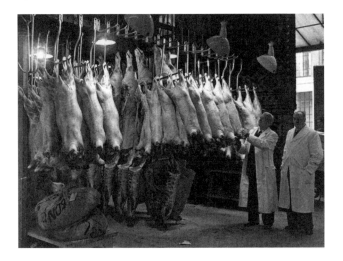

The tale of the three little pigs is well known but if you, in your idle moments, dear reader, imagined that the pigs lived happily ever after, you are very much mistaken. There are of course different versions of our tale, some sanitized for children in which the first two little pigs escape being eaten, and rewritings in which the big bad wolf is painted as victim rather than aggressor. Well, I can tell you that those first two little pigs did indeed survive, scurrying over to the third pig's house to watch the wolf puff ineffectually at a brick wall and then tumble down the chimney into a cauldron of boiling water. They survived, grew plump, and in the course of time, spawned many offspring, thereby establishing the House of Straw and the House of Twigs. Who am I? As you have probably guessed, perceptive reader, I am a descendant of the House of Brick, scion of the third pig who finally put an end to the big bad wolf.

The tale I am about to relate concerns frying pans and fires, towers, and the drawbacks of ascribing facile adjectives to complex characters. The wolf, as it turned out in the scheme of things, was not so much 'big' and 'bad' as 'instinctual' and 'naïve'. Indeed, our encounter with the wolf prepared us well for our subsequent exploits with humankind.

We have coexisted for a long time, the families Suidae and Sapien. Man has hunted and butchered us, fashioned raiment from our skins and subjugated us. We in turn have fed them, clothed them and played the role of their pets. Not exactly a quid pro quo. They come for us without warning – there is no 'little pig, little pig, let me in', just a bolt gun or a clean sharp cut to the throat. No house, made of brick or otherwise, is sufficiently sturdy to keep them out. Here in the City of London, we have been slaughtered at Smoothfield livestock market for over a thousand years. This accursed ground has changed greatly over the centuries – for a start, it's now called Smithfield – but its purpose, the slaughter and trade of livestock, has been cruelly unrelenting. Where in the early days we were herded down these thoroughfares in droves or ferried

Restrictions had been laid down as
long ago as the 14th Century to ensure
the remainder of the capital would be
174   free of livestock.

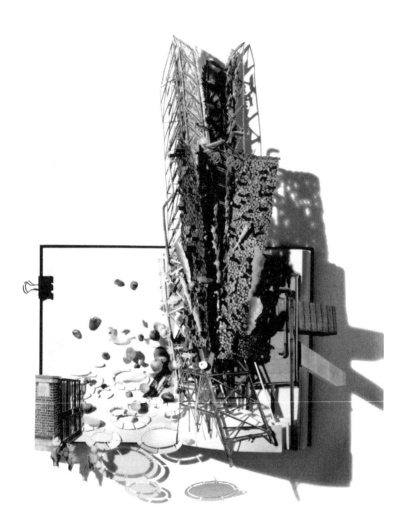

down the river, we are now driven by lorry to the butcher's block. The grazing pastures and water from the Fleet that rendered the land so appropriate for its function have since been covered over with asphalt and two sprawling buildings separated by a grand boulevard of cast iron arches. Cowcross street and Cock Lane still exist, but Pheasant Court, Duck Lane and Goose Alley have been relegated to the annals of history.

To state the obvious, enduring horrific living conditions only to be killed and eaten is no laughing matter. Three years ago, a conclave was called to see what could be done about our predicament. After much lengthy and heated debate, it was decided that we would send a delegation to the human government to plead our case. There were those who branded our proposed undertaking futile, but as Grandmother Pig used to say, 'Whatever you do, do it the best you can because that's the way to get along in the world.'

The representative put forward by the House of Straw was a creative type, and elected to approach the Ministry of Culture. He was ushered into a plush and opulent room smelling of books and old wealth where he expounded our grievances to the Minister. In the corner sat a fat man with a very red face, a small goatee beard and a factotum who took notes throughout the meeting. In

At the feet of the three towers lies an orchard from which the most mouth-watering scents from myriad varieties of apple emanate.

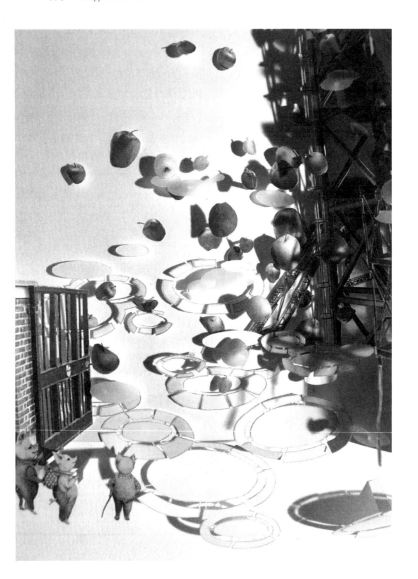

Air flows through the straw bale walls, caressing pig carcasses on its way before dissipating through the roof.

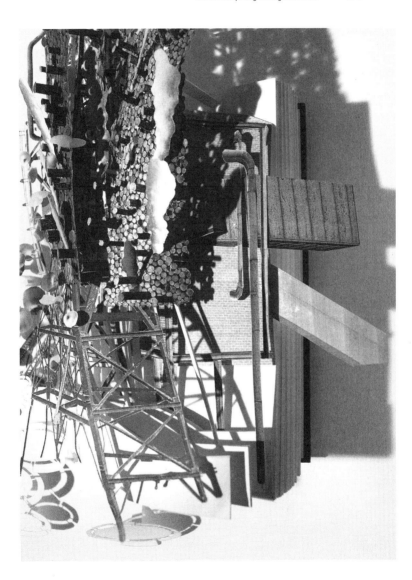

A second tower, this time built of sticks, was erected in the east corner of Smithfield, a lattice structure of apple, maple and alder wood.

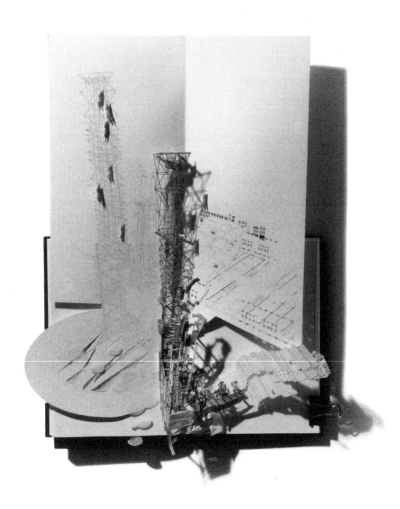

exchange for the freedom of the Straw clan, the little pig offered the Minister unlimited image rights of our kind. Man would be free to use our likenesses in animated features, soft plush toys and any merchandise they wished to teach their children numeracy and how to read their ABCs. The Minister listened to what the pig had to say, nodding sagely at the appropriate moments. By the end of the meeting, the factotum had drawn up a contract setting out the proposed articles of agreement and asked the pig to sign. The Minister then shook the little pig's trotter and led him to a small chamber that was neither plush nor opulent but would be the poor delegate's home for the remainder of his short short life. In the other room, the fat man with the goatee calmly fed the contract, ink still wet, into the roaring log fire behind him.

In ironic commemoration of this meeting between our two species, the Ministry erected a tower of straw at Smithfield that you can now see looming over the north corner of Horace Jones' Italianate buildings that date from the mid 19th Century. Why Smithfield? Perhaps it is because Death's spectre already hangs heavy over this hectare of land. It has ever been a stage for barbarous activity, and not only directed to the four-legged kind – warring humans have been executed, stabbed and even boiled in cauldrons of oil here, so where better to erect a shrine to the Grim Reaper?

Painted shadows wrap Smithfield, mimicking those cast by the towers during the day which the night porters never experience.

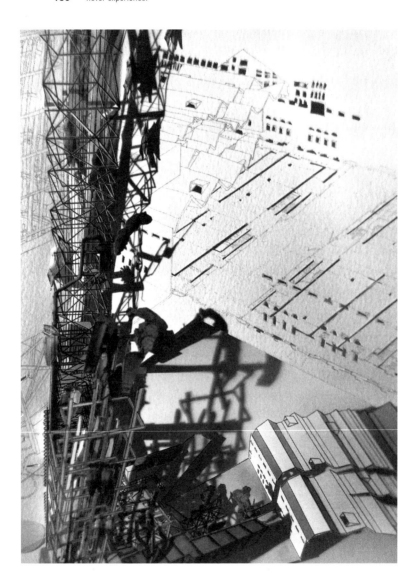

Since that time, the Tower of Straw has been a repository for our carcasses, smoked and flavoured with the chippings from apple, maple and alder trees. Air flows through the straw bale walls and wafts through the tower's lofty core, caressing our flayed bodies on its way before dissipating through the roof. The soot, grease and moisture amassing on the underside of the roof binds the straw together, keeping our precious flesh, and the porters that handle our corpses, protected from the elements.

When it became clear that their champion would not be returning, the House of Straw entreated their cousins at the House of Sticks to send their own envoy. The delegate from the Second House was a scientific type and elected to approach the Ministry of Health. Although the departmental buildings and the Minister were different, the fat man and his factotum were again in attendance. They listened as the second pig offered the Minister an annual donation of pig organs and cells for xerotransplantation in exchange for the freedom of her clan. Pig cells, she argued, were compatible with the human body but were free of viruses and pathogens that could be spread from primate donors, making them ideal for use in humans with deficient bodily functions. She reasoned to herself that if the genetic bonds between human and pigkind could be recognized and strengthened, we would be less likely to be seen as

The tower is continuously under construction as the uppermost storeys are constantly whittled away to smoke bacon and ham in the Tower of Straw.

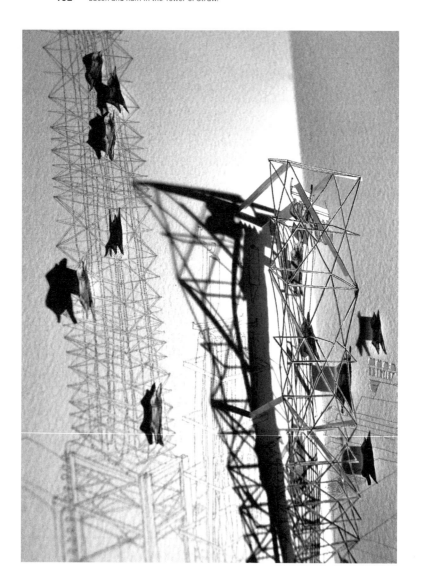

nutritional fodder thanks to the humans' aversion to cannibalism. The pig's case was both cogent and impassioned but her fate was no different from her predecessor's. A contract was signed and burned, and the wretched swine was not eaten but rendered into fertilizer, chinny chin chin and all, in deference to her arguments. A second tower, this time built of sticks, was erected in the east corner of Smithfield, a lattice structure of apple, maple and alder wood. The tower is continuously under construction as the uppermost storeys are constantly whittled away to smoke bacon and ham in the Tower of Straw. The lattice is slowly winched up on a rotating cam and a new timber podium built beneath it to keep the tower at the height agreed by the planning authority of Islington.

And so it fell to me, representative of the House of Bricks, to speak to mankind. I am neither cultured nor a creature of science. If pushed, I would probably describe myself as pragmatic and matter-of-fact. The government department I sought out was naturally therefore the Ministry of Agriculture, the very department responsible for our unfortunate plight. After the initial introductions, the first thing I said to the Minister was that humans would always see our kind as food for their plates. I told him that I would not be so jejune as to petition for a stay of execution, a pronouncement that coaxed a raised eyebrow on the face of the goateed man standing in the

Cowcross street and Cock Lane still exist, but Pheasant Court, Duck Lane and Goose Alley have been relegated to the annals of history.

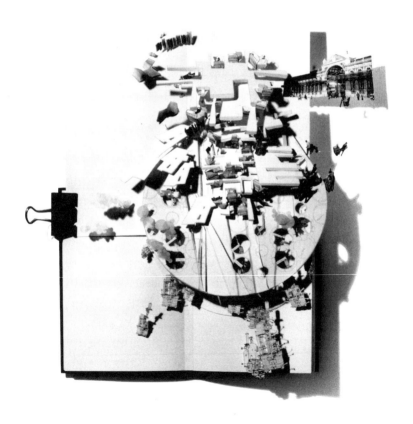

shadows. It is the fate of all living creatures to perish, and we are all, humans included, but fragile links in the food chain; each of us can only hope to better our existence. With this in mind, I reminded him of mankind's responsibilities as our custodians as well as our executioners. Their acts of genocide must come at a price – that of our wellbeing. No contract was signed. None needed to be. The Minister of Agriculture showed me to the door and I never saw him or the other man again.

Unique amongst world cities, London has a meat market at its heart, but it exists only under the sufferance of its denizens; indeed restrictions had been laid down as long ago as the 14th Century to ensure the remainder of the capital would be free of livestock. Inhumane death, effluvia, rotting carcasses and nervous terror benefit no one.

It therefore came to pass that a third and final tower was erected, this time constructed from brick, in which we have sanctuary during the day. Any butchery is now limited to the hours between midnight and dawn, an amnesty existing outside these hours during which we may eat and slumber undisturbed. The meat porters sleep with us in the tower, feed us properly and regularly clean out our stalls. We live each day as it comes and are slaughtered by the same

The meat porters sleep with us in the
tower, feed us properly and regularly
186   clean out our stalls.

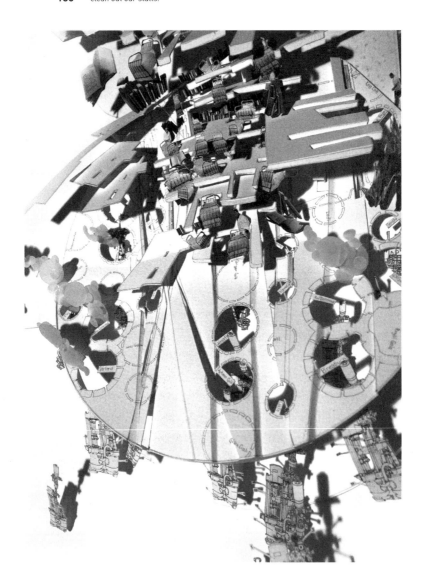

hands that feed us.

Locked in a nocturnal existence, we and the porters occupy a different world from those outside the tower. We hear that in the centre of the market is a kitchen serving an all-pork menu. The seating to the connecting restaurant spills outside to encompass the Central London Markets and its surrounding roofscape. From here, the porters can see a painted shadow wrapping Smithfield. This is the shadow of the three towers cast during the day, a sight the night porters never experience. At the feet of the three towers lies an orchard from which the most mouth-watering scents from myriad varieties of apple emanate, feeding our daytime dreams. At night, the apples are scentless. There are rumours that the orchard contains no fruit but releases atomized smell particles triggered by the sun's shadow. If this is true, man's folly knows no bounds.

This, then, is the way we live, receiving a pound of feed by day, sacrificing a pound of flesh by night. What's that? Monstrous you say? A traitor to my own kind? No, heartless reader, you are in no position to cast aspersions. We are not friends, you and I. You are the fat man with the goatee beard. I am but a pragmatist, making my way as best I can. That's the only way to get along in the world.

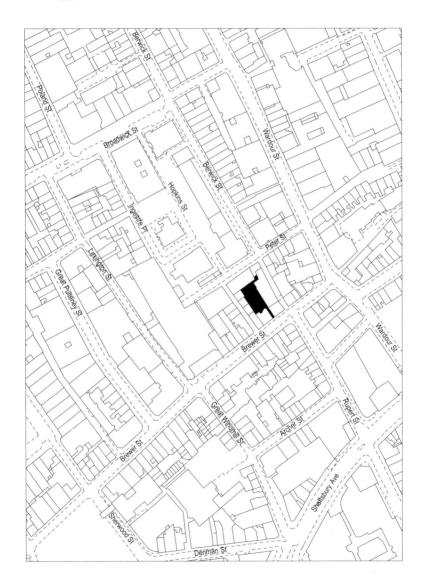

W 1
The Baker's Garden

The Baker's Garden

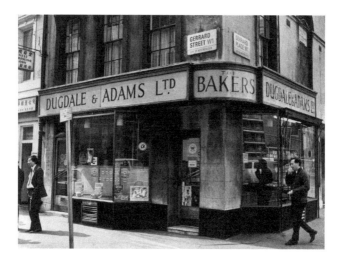

The clock strikes three and the Baker's garden begins to coalesce. Located on the south side of Soho Fields, the garden is an oasis concealed by its fleeting nature and the cover of darkness as much as geographical location. Known and enjoyed by an intimate handful of local residents, it is in this respect not unlike the private members clubs that will later proliferate in Soho, but unlike these establishments, its membership is made up of the dispossessed and eccentric rather than the well-heeled and bourgeois.

An hour earlier, the baker, who is the custodian of the garden, rose from his slumber, nudged off his bed by the steady pressure of sourdough starter straining against the lid of the bins on which he slept. The starter is like a child around which his life revolves. It had been nurtured and fed by his family for generations, every day without fail. The baker rests only when the bread rests; when it rises, so does he.

The baker's father, grandfather and great-grandfather had all been bakers. Descended from an old Huguenot family, the baker had shown a talent for making bread from an early age. Merely flour and water, bread was a simple amalgamation of two everyday ingredients, leavened with a sprinkling of airborne magic that his compatriot, Pasteur, had named yeast a few decades ago. These invisible organisms would breathe life into the mixture, imbuing it with bubbles, aroma and taste, ballooning its volume fourfold in the process. The young baker had instinctively known the perfect moment to add the salt that would extinguish life from the yeast and capture the dough at its apogee of form, texture and elasticity. Flour, water. Yeast. Warmth. Breath. Life. Growth. Salt. Death. Yes, the alchemical process of breadmaking had come effortlessly to the precocious youth, although his experiments in the Compton Street House, leaving a trail of sticky detritus in his wake, had driven his mother to apoplexies of rage. She would discover globules and

And so into being came the baker's garden – a glorious landscape of smells shifting from fermenting acidity to caramelizing sweetness ...

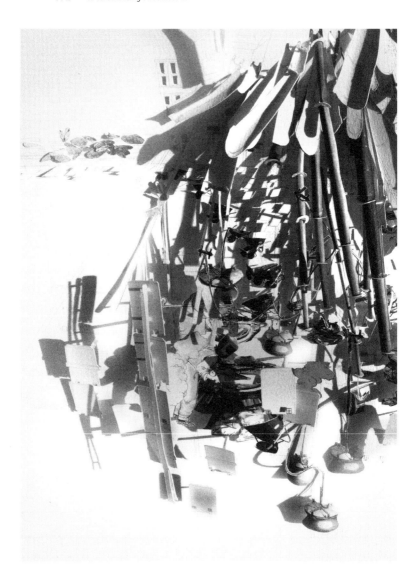

... a riot of auburn and amber reflecting
the fires of the bakery and street lamps
outside, a symphony of hissing steam
and the pummelling of dough.

193

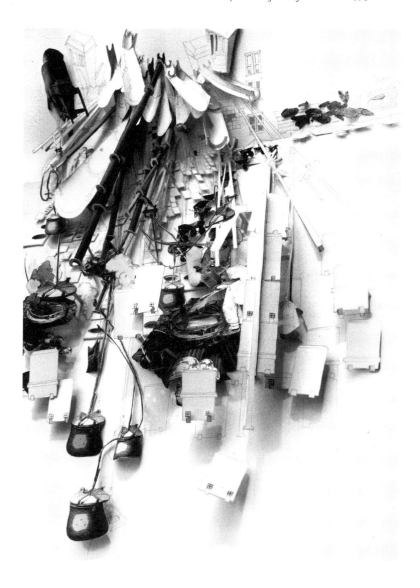

Space was stolen from the street by
quilting the pavement with clay ovens
that would be hoisted up by a trellis of
194   pulleys during the hours of light.

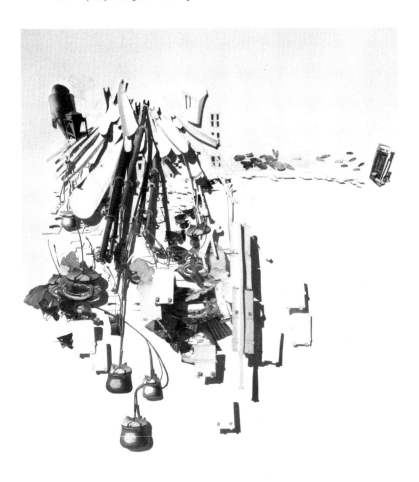

splatters of bubbling mix secreted in the pantry, under the beds, in the coal store and all over the family cat's paws. At dawn, his father would empty his son's loaves out of their wicker bannetons, slash their tops with a well-practised curlicue, and give them pride of place in the centre of the wood-burning stove. At breakfast, he would grudgingly concede that his son's sourdough, with its beautiful crust and fine-grained texture, reached sublime heights that his never would.

Great things were expected of the baker when he took over the family business, but something unexpected had transpired – the panoply of brioche, bloomers, bâtons and boules that the adult baker sold in his shop were poor things – unsatisfactory in appearance, texture and all-round gustatory experience. The panniers at the end of each day would remain full, and his purse empty.

Contrary to the gossip of his customers and dwindling social circle, the baker had not tired of his métier. If anything, his obsession had grown, its focus sharpened. To the bafflement of his friends, the baker had channelled all his artistry into process rather than the product; whether the bread was fit for consumption had become an irrelevance. He would say, 'even a baker cannot live by bread alone', explaining that in every painting, building, symphony or human life,

There was a truthfulness and honesty
about the smells, light and warmth that
emanated from the garden deriving
from their natural function.

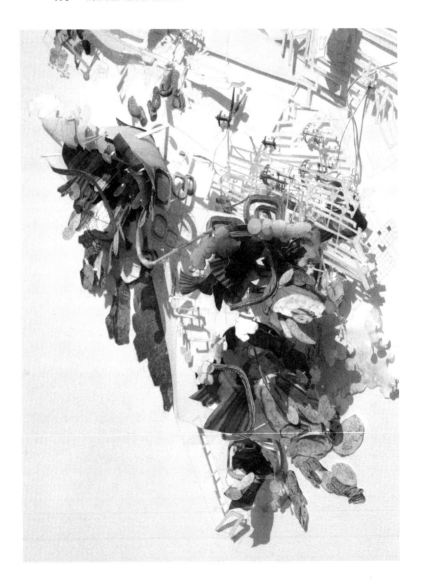

there were fugitive moments of raw grace and gestural purity that refinement and over-polishing could only dilute.

And so into being came the baker's garden – a glorious landscape of smells shifting from fermenting acidity to caramelizing sweetness, a riot of auburn and amber reflecting the fires of the bakery and street lamps outside, a symphony of hissing steam and the pummelling of dough.

While the baker delighted in his synaesthetic pleasure dome, he was saddened to be its only witness and resolved to share his rapture. In order to magnify the scale of his garden, he enlisted the aid of a young inventor in Islington named Robinson who explained to him the principles of pulleys, cams, pistons and gears. Together, they overhauled the property, stealing space from the street by quilting the pavement with clay ovens that would be hoisted up by a trellis of pulleys that would leave the ground clear during the hours of light. Water collected from the roof's pantiles would cascade onto the hot terracotta below, creating topiaries of steam that assumed the form of nebulous chimaeras. There was a truthfulness and honesty about the smells, light and warmth that emanated from the garden deriving from natural function beyond the scope of the finest perfume, lamp or radiator.

The topiaries of water vapour will become indistinguishable from clouds, the play of shadows from the oven flame will fade in the dawning light.

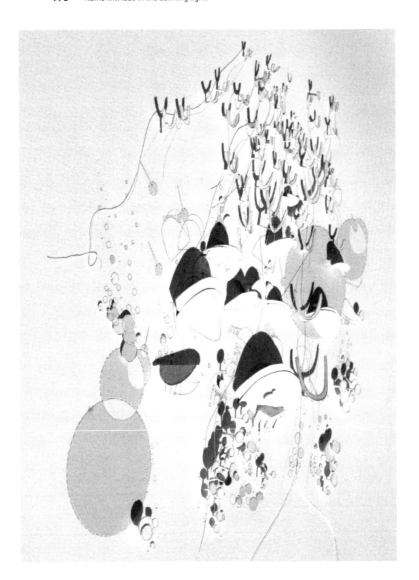

As the ephemeral field expanded, the garden began to attract a mixture of peripatetic visitors and local misfits who came to decipher the excitations of taste, smell and temperature penetrating the fabric of the neighbourhood. Rimbaud and Verlaine were known to frequent the garden, declaring that the atmosphere was conducive to the creation of verse, although usually after having been ejected from the Greek Street Tavern.

It is now the end of the fourth watch, and the sun will soon rise, triggering the dematerialization of the garden. The topiaries of water vapour will become indistinguishable from clouds, the play of shadows from the oven flame will fade in the dawning light, and the rhythmic pounding of the dough become so much white noise within Soho's bustle. The garden's itinerant visitors will wake up in the street, wondering if the nocturnal oasis had been merely a mirage fuelled by absinthe or opiates. Night watchmen, gamblers, privy-men, prostitutes and punters will withdraw to their lodgings, ceding the city to the day folk and leaving genteel London to its respectable activities. And the baker will sit patiently in his empty shop, counting the hours until his garden flowers again.

Water collected from the roof's pantiles would cascade onto the hot terracotta below, creating nebulous columns of steam.

200

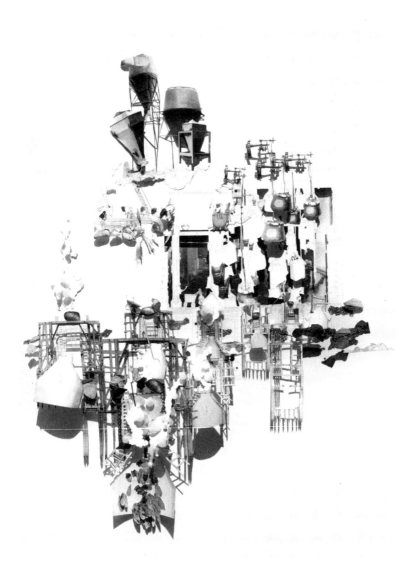

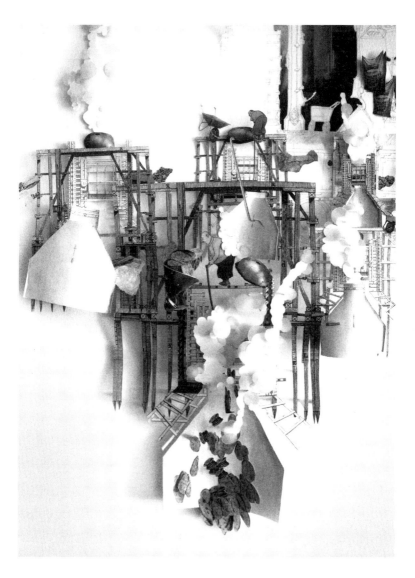

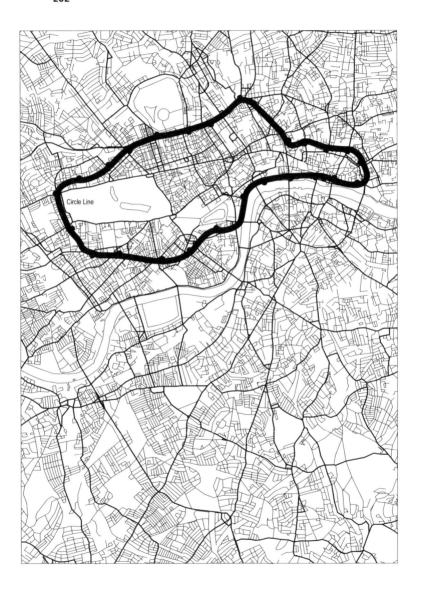

W 2 t o E C 3

The Celestial River

The Celestial River

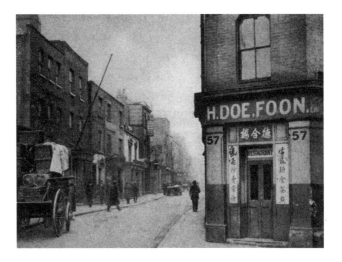

In 1736 a massive flood led to the Westbourne bursting its banks and the whole of the area south of the Serpentine down through Albert Gate, through Knightsbridge and Belgravia was under several feet of water for weeks. The Thames waterman made most of an opportunity and rowed sightseers from Chelsea up to Knightsbridge and beyond. At this time most of the roads around London were impassable to wheeled vehicles for most of the year anyway so the sudden appearance of extra water for boat travel – always the preferred mode of transport for Londoners – made Hyde Park far more popular than it would otherwise have been.

- 'London's Strangest Tales', Tom Quinn, 2008

The young orphan Wong was raised on the dragonboats of the Celestial River. Afflicted by a large red mark on the side of his face, the boy suffered from taunts and mockery from those around him. The pale-faced native boys would tug on his pigtail, impersonate his Oriental features by pinching the skin around their eyes, and ridicule the Pidgin English he spoke. However, the barbs either missed their mark or were accepted with calm equanimity, angering Wong's would-be tormentors all the more. Apparently oblivious, he would simply carry on with whatever he was doing with sombre imperturbability. Wong was treated no better by his fellow countrymen from Shanghai who lived in a separate enclave at Pennyfields. Persecution by the white devils he could understand, brainwashed as they were by stories of the villainous Fu Manchu in which all Chinamen were cunning, corrupting London's good honest citizens with opiates in sordid dens of vice; the Shanghainese, despite their differences in dialect and culture, should, he felt, be brothers in adversity.

Wong's father, a seaman from Canton, had arrived during the first wave of the Chinese Diaspora following the Taiping rebellion and the Treaty of Nanking that had opened up China to British trade. Wong's mother had died bearing him into this life, and as soon as his

As the storm grew into a whirlwind, a waterspout erupted from the Thames below, transforming into Tian Long, the great Celestial Dragon.

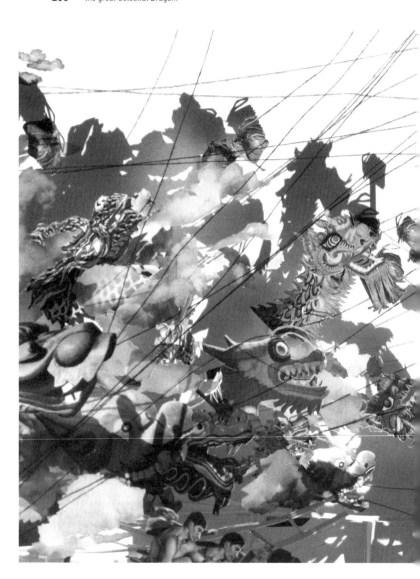

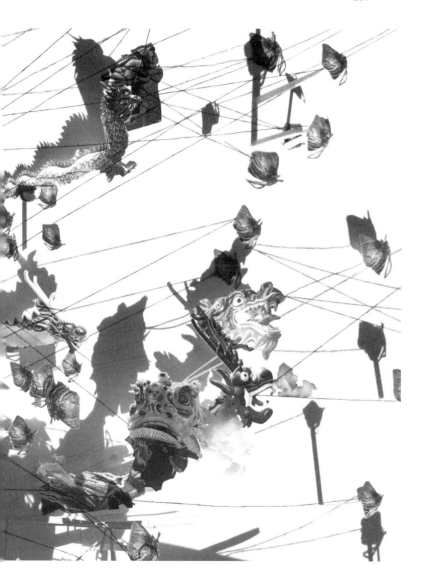

Flames billowed from the Dragon King's nostrils, flaring into great columns of steam.

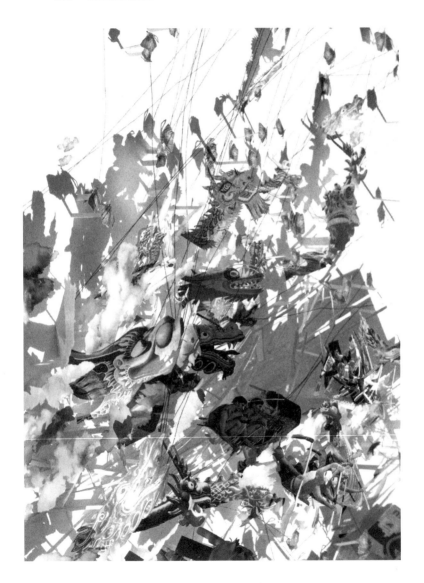

son could stand on his own two legs, the elder Wong signed aboard the 'Bulysses' as a Lascar for the East India Tea Company with the boy in tow, bringing tea, silk and ceramics to the Royal Albert Docks in London. Obedient, hard working and willing to work for low wages, Wong's father and compatriots from Canton had found it easy to find work. Father and son had lived in the squalid and cramped conditions of Ah Tack's Lodging House in the Limehouse Causeway. There were no Chinese women in this Chinatown, not even in the laundry houses where lime was used to bleach clothes white, leaving the itinerant sailors free to while away their spare hours gambling.

In the evenings, when the elder Wong was not playing pak-kop-piu, he would regale his son with stories involving dragons, gods and talking animals, explaining that the Han people understood elemental forces through folktales that had been passed down through countless generations. As they travelled the seven seas, the Chinese would weave tales around every unusual landscape feature they came across, aiding navigation while teaching the values of virtuousness, duty and probity. Mountains, rivers, caves and later cities would become bound by the legends woven into their fabric, living on in the memories and imaginations of both natives and visiting foreigners.

Wong had just guided the boat out of Bayswater station, keeping the sweep oar straight and true despite the buffeting winds.

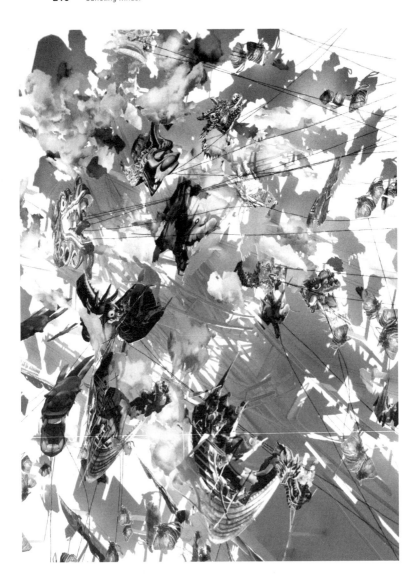

Despite poverty and its attendant hardships, father and son enjoyed their odd moments of happiness until the elder Wong was forcibly repatriated back to the Orient. Receiving a tip-off from a Hindoo Lascar that the local constabulary were coming for him, he bundled his son into Lee's Opium Parlour, leaving Young Wong with only a jade necklace that had belonged to his mother and a promise to return as soon as he could.

And so Young Wong became Orphan Wong. Before long, the boy discovered that he could best conceal himself from the attention of the authorities on the Celestial River, a transport system in the sky that circumnavigated the city of London. Although the heavens are boundless, the Celestial River flows along a prescribed cloud path, steering clear of the heavenly palaces in which the Bodhisattva Kuan Yin and other deities reside. Five leagues in circumference, the river is traversed by 44 teak longboats, powered by the passengers who paddle against the clouds. The route passes through 27 stations including the Temple where offerings of flowers, fruit and incense are made daily, the station of the Black Friar, the Moor's Gate and the Tower Gateway. Each station, of course, has its own tale to tell, and Orphan Wong, the eternal passenger, knew them all by heart.

The dragonboat in which Wong stowed himself was helmed by a

Five leagues in circumference, the
river is traversed by 44 teak longboats,
powered by the passengers who paddle
against the clouds.

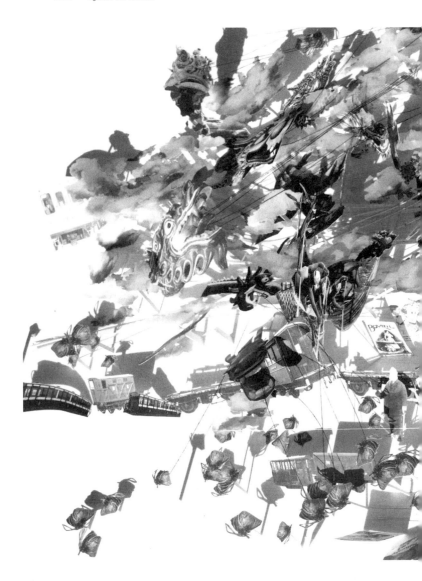

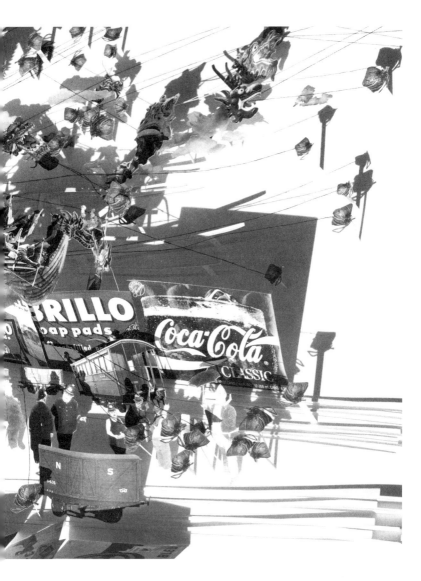

The drummer increased the cadence
of his beat, exhorting the boat's crew
214   to redouble their efforts.

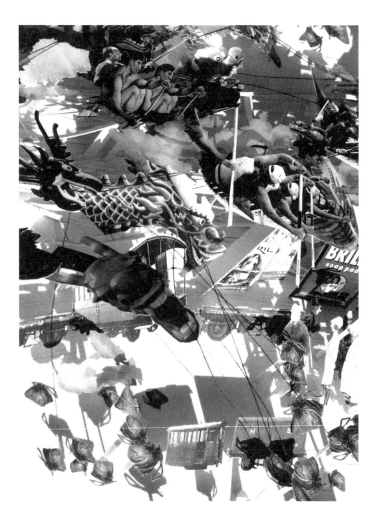

sweepsman who more often than not turned a blind eye to the waif's continued presence. A lazy man, the sweep would allow Wong to cover his position at the tiller in exchange for a half-eaten morsel or the odd halfpenny while he chewed on tarry opium residue.

It was during one such instance on the fifth day of the fifth lunar month, the solstice, that a great storm cloud appeared on the horizon. Wong had just guided the boat out of Bayswater station, keeping the sweep oar straight and true despite the buffeting winds. Taking his cue, the drummer increased the cadence of his beat, exhorting the boat's crew to redouble their efforts.

'The Dragon King is vengeful,' said the sweepsman. 'It is said he is searching for his missing daughter.' As the storm grew into a whirlwind, a waterspout erupted from the Thames below, transforming into Tian Long, the great Celestial Dragon. Tian Long was terrible to behold, with his camel head, demon eyes, eagle claws and serpentine neck. His golden scales, numbering nine times nine, glistened brightly in the rain. Vessels fell from the sky, crashing past the windows of the Georgian townhouses and slum housing below until but one longboat remained afloat, knifing through the gale and fog. Young Wong's hand on the tiller never wavered; his sober eyes never left the horizon. Tian Long,

The route passes through 27 stations including the Temple, the station of the Black Friar, the Moor's Gate and the Tower Gateway.

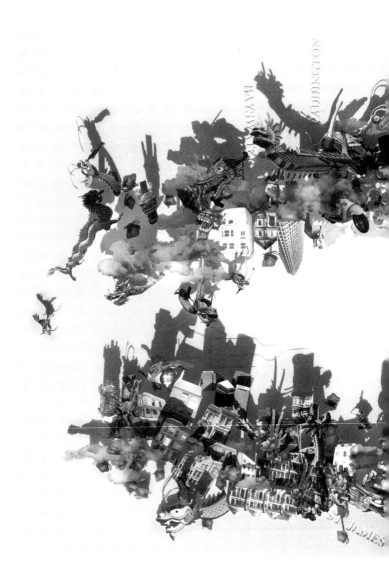

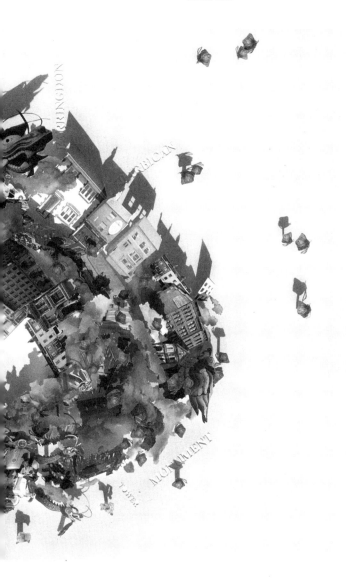

Wong discovered that he could best conceal himself on the Celestial River, a transport system in the sky that circumnavigated the city of London.

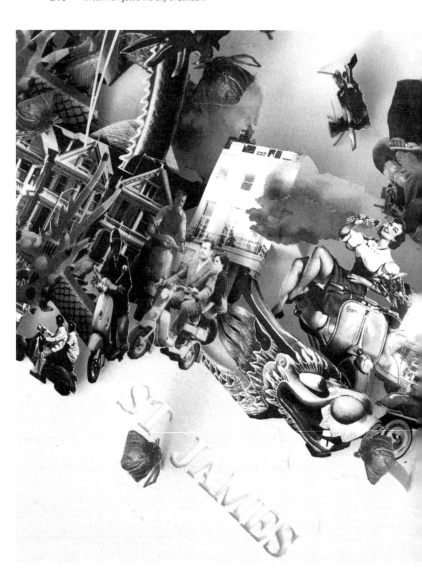

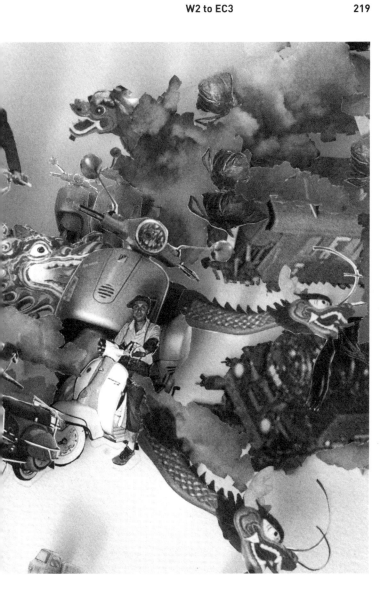

Although the heavens are boundless, the Celestial River flows along a prescribed cloud path, steering clear of the heavenly palaces.

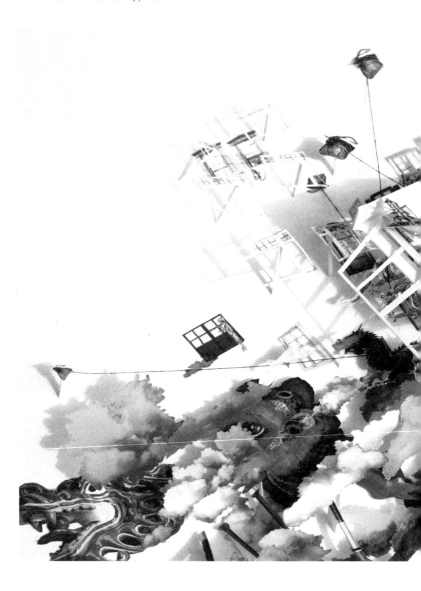

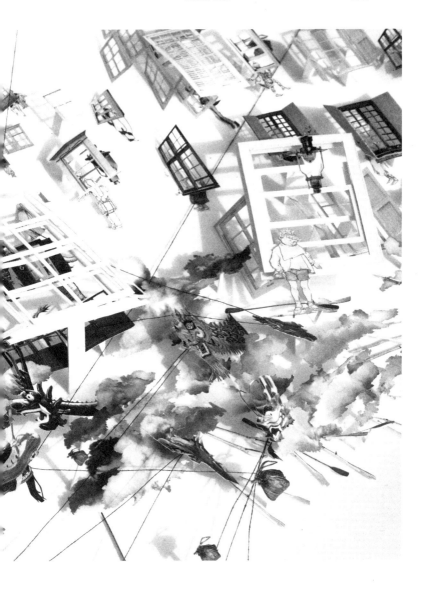

furious, sucked in his cheeks and spat fire. Flames billowed from the Dragon King's nostrils, flaring into great columns of steam.

'Who dares defy the will of the Dragon King?' roared Tian Long. Young Wong quietly stood, his hand keeping the oar steady while the crew cowered in the hull.

'Impetuous youth! I will rend the flesh from your bones. I will ...' Tian Long, the celestial dragon drew back, his whiskers flailing in the wind. 'How is it that you bear the mark of my daughter on your face? To which mortal clan do you belong?' demanded the Dragon King.

'Reverend Sir, my family name is Wong. My father has been banished from Albion for many a long year and my mother died when I was born. I have but this keepsake to remind me of her,' said Young Wong, raising the jade necklace from his neck.

Tears flowed from the great dragon's eyes. 'My daughter's son,' cried Tian Long. 'I have searched the seven seas for sign of Chih Nu for seven long years. Now I hear she has departed this life, but joy tempers my grief as I behold you, blood of my blood.'

'The next station is Kings Cross. Please change here for the District, Northern, Piccadilly line and National Rail services.'

'Billy! Wake up! We have to change here,' said Mrs Wong. 'Come on, chop chop! We're already late for dim sum with your Aunt.'

'Where are we going, Mum?'

'The New World, silly boy. The same place we always go,' said Mrs Wong.

Vessels fell from the sky, crashing past the windows of the Georgian townhouses and slum housing below.

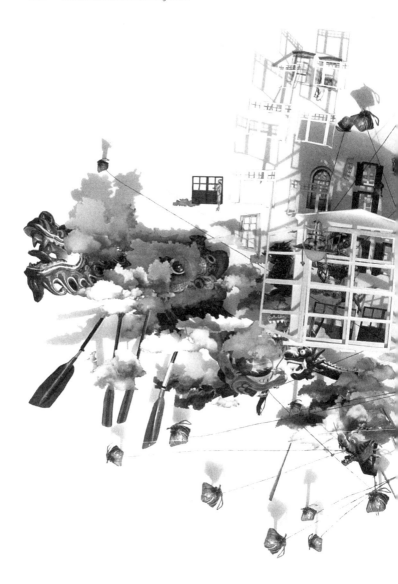

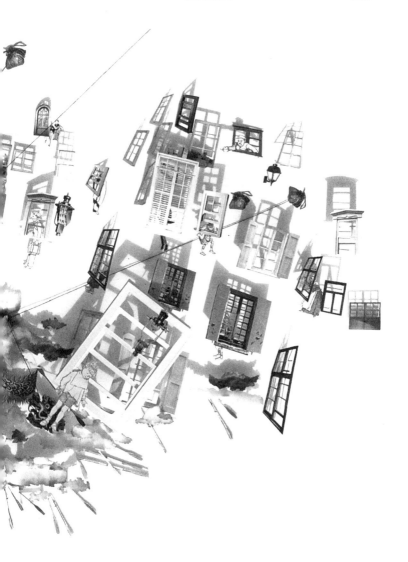

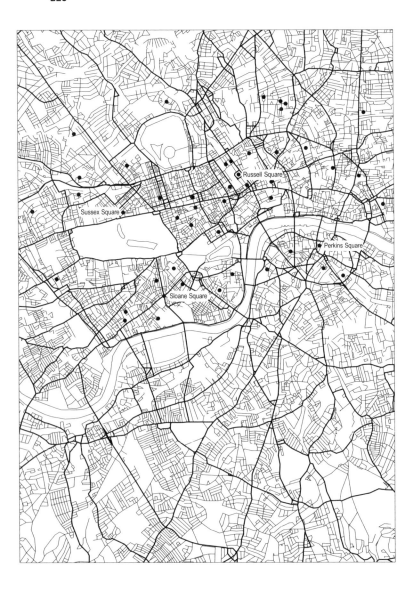

Russell Square

Sussex Square

Perkins Square

Sloane Square

ANY
PUBLIC SQUARE
IN LONDON

The Globetrotter

The Globetrotter

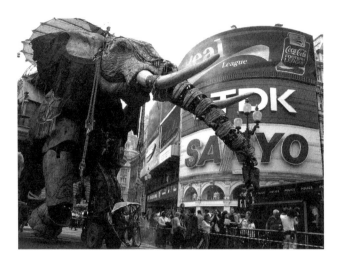

A giant suitcase stands unattended along the Thames Path at the end of Clink Street. A crowd gathers, pondering its significance. The case measures eight metres long by four metres wide and is the height of a small two-storey house. It possesses no windows or doors, so is unlikely to function as a residence. There are no seams to the leather-like material that covers the case, and no animal that could give up a hide of such proportions. The protective corners and handle, which are made of hard tanned leather, make the object immediately recognizable as a Globetrotter suitcase, and bear evidence of wear in scuffs and abrasions. Adhered to the surface of the case are labels, as one might expect to find on a piece of luggage. A man in the crowd reckons that the case is approximately twelve times larger than a conventional piece of luggage, the same ratio by which Lemuel Gulliver dwarfs the miniature race of people he encounters in Swift's Menippean satire, but London is no Lilliput and this is no literary fancy.

Unbeknownst to this group of observers, the globetrotter is always transported in the early hours of morning under the cover of darkness. Carried on an articulated lorry, it is deposited on unfamiliar ground, sometimes on its base, sometimes laid flat, with no suggestion of the enchanting spatial wizardry that will dramatically unfurl from its interior. The Globetrotter, which takes its name from its form, is a peripatetic stage that opens up and reconfigures depending on its locale and designated pro tem function.

At midmorning, a stage crew arrives. With the aid of pulleys, winches and a phalanx of powerfully built men, the case is opened and the components extracted. Due to the manifold ways in which its basic structure can be rearranged and the flair with which the crew works, the installation of the theatre is a spectacle in itself. Open and upturned, the Globetrotter has manifested as a pop-up

The Globetrotter is deposited on unfamiliar ground with no suggestion of the enchanting spatial wizardry that will dramatically unfurl from its interior.

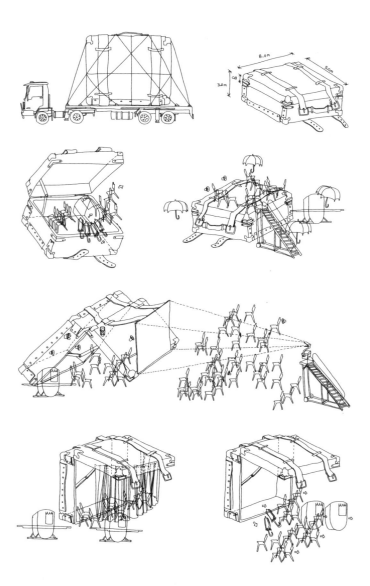

cinema, catching commuters unaware to tarry at the spectacle of light coalescing to tell a story instead of resuming their evening journey home. Other times, the suitcase remains shut, operating as a bandstand or a stage for Hindustani Ragas and ceremonial addresses. Most often, however, the case is seen standing on its base with its lid, housing a lighting rig, projecting out to cover a stage. In this guise, it has hosted community meetings, operettas, weddings, plays and gallery openings. In each instance, the reordering of public space appropriates the spatial and textural characteristics of its host environment, whether employing a Georgian terrace as a theatrical backdrop, lamp posts as struts or street furniture as props, a process that sublimates the familiar into the uncanny.

Open-air theatres of the 16th Century originally were built with south-facing aspects to better light the features of the players; the Globetrotter, being a more mobile construct, rotates its orientation to best suit the time of day and proximity of neighbouring buildings. An intricate system of reflectors soften the light according to mood, operated by skilled lighting designers who deftly cope with, and capitalize on, the country's mercurial changes in weather and cloud cover.

While its main components are often deployed around the

A cloud of red umbrellas lit from
beneath glow like lanterns and keep
232 the audience dry in the autumn rain.

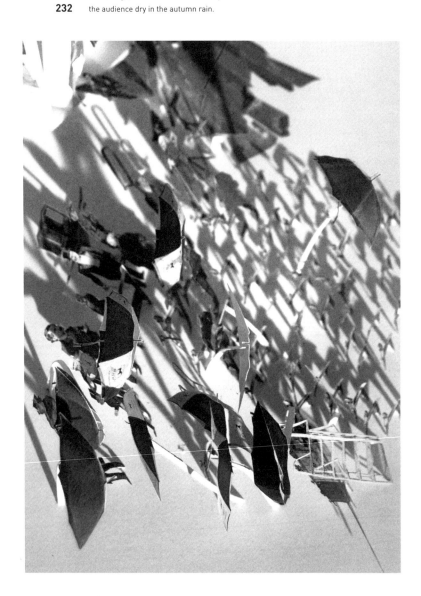

Globetrotter case to establish a fluid curtilage, dressing rooms, technical equipment and storage areas are neatly concealed within the depths of its structure. Seating arrangements may be formal for official events or ad hoc to encourage intimate engagement, blurring the boundary between spectator and performer. This particular evening, with the Thames and a replica of the Golden Hind forming the backdrop, spectators are seated in sparse groupings for a Cantonese opera, allowing the musicians and actors to weave around and immerse themselves into the audience. The story tells the tale of an orphan who encounters a celestial dragon searching for his lost daughter, only to discover that the missing woman is his mother who died giving birth to him. A cloud of red umbrellas lit from beneath glow like lanterns and keep the audience dry in the autumn rain as the lighting crew contrive to transform the drizzling rain into a diaphanous mist through which the bamboo and canvas dragon materializes.

In former times, the public spaces of London themselves constituted a vast theatre, from Punch and Judy shows in the square to Shakespearean plays performed on floating barges to crowds on the banks of the Thames, or more bleakly, the real life travails of beggars and itinerants with no walls to conceal their personal dramas behind. Contemporary London is not only a different time,

The main components are deployed around the Globetrotter case to establish a fluid curtilage.

but a different place, purged for the most part equally of vagrants and serendipitous amusement. The Globetrotter is therefore a welcome anachronism, eschewing digital slickness for steampunk stylings; its mechanics are redolent of Pugin's Daguerre-type Diorama at Regents Park where a rotating arena and elaborate reflected lighting would transform a flat painting into a three-dimensional

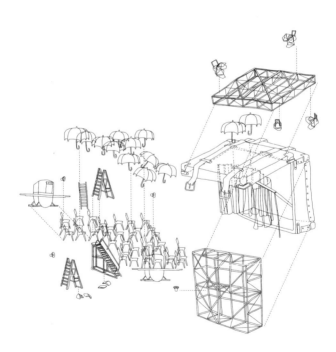

environment of wind, light and atmosphere. Where such mechanics were synchronous with Victorian Britain, however, many of these contrivances, rediscovered by the Globetrotter, have a newfound power to beguile and confound 21st Century audiences.

The origins of the theatre are unclear and are perhaps intentionally suppressed to further the Globetrotter's mystique. Some have argued that the theatre might be an homage to the short-lived Roost, a Gentlemen's Club that occupied a small plot on Pall Mall during the latter days of the 19th Century, but the presiding opinion is that the theatre is a marketing tool devised by the eponymous luggage company. Whatever its provenance, it should be celebrated for disrupting the mundane, and reclaiming the noble art of street theatre from pedestrian mime artists as well as public space from drunken revellers at night.

Over time, the stiff shell of the Globetrotter accumulates labels, press cuttings and advertisements, bearing witness to the places it has travelled and the events to which it has played host. This patina, effectively a history of the theatre's voyage through London and other locations throughout the world, becomes so encrusted that the gargantuan suitcase cannot be strapped shut, whereupon the covering is excised and archived at the Globetrotter Museum.

This patina constitutes a history of the theatre's voyage through London and other locations throughout the world.

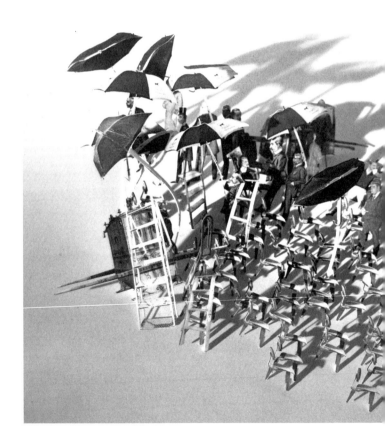

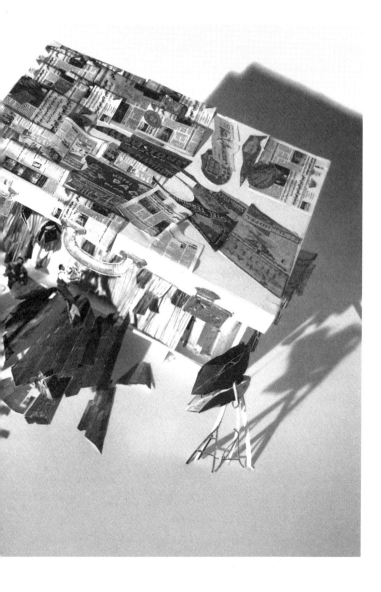

Project + Reproduction Credits

PROLOGUE: Dream Isle
2008; design team: CJ Lim/Studio 8 Architects with Thomas Hillier, Maxwell Mutanda, Rachel Guo, Ed Liu

NW1: A Midsummer Night's Dream
2009; design team: CJ Lim/Studio 8 Architects with Pascal Bronner

SE1 to EC4: Discontinuous Cities
2007; design team: CJ Lim/Studio 8 Architects with Maxwell Mutanda, Tomasz Marchewka

SE16: Darwin's Islands
2008; design team: CJ Lim/Studio 8 Architects with Maxwell Mutanda, Jacqueline Chak

SW1: Madame Delia's Urban Roost
2007; design team: CJ Lim/Studio 8 Architects with Maxwell Mutanda, Chris Lees

SW7: Carousel
2010; design team: CJ Lim/Studio 8 Architects with Maxwell Mutanda

SW11: Battersea Dating Agency
2006; design team: CJ Lim/Studio 8 Architects with Jimmy Hung

EC1: The Nocturnal Tower
2007; design team: CJ Lim/Studio 8 Architects with Barry Cho

W1: The Baker's Garden
2008; design team: CJ Lim/Studio 8 Architects with Safia Qureshi

W2 to EC3: The Celestial River
2007; design team: CJ Lim/Studio 8 Architects with Maxwell Mutanda, Sarah Custance

ANY PUBLIC SQUARE IN LONDON: The Globetrotter
2007; design team: CJ Lim/Studio 8 Architects with Maxwell Mutanda, Cynthia Leung, Tomasz Marchewka

Reproduction Credits

22–23 Panorama from Primrose Hill (Paul Allen)

62 Playboy Bunnies Collecting for Charity (Popperfoto / Getty Images)

84 The Frost Fair of 1683, River Thames

98 Iceberg with Polar Bear on Thames (Shaun Curry / AFP / Getty Images)

112 Plan of Reform Club, Pall Mall (Sir Charles Barry)

130 Horse Overlooking St Paul's from A Multi-storey Stable (George Reid / Museum of London / Heritage Images)

148 Battersea Dogs Home (The Lordprice Collection)

172 Meat at Smithfield (Monty Fresco / Getty Images)

190 Bakery at Gerard Street (Mike Lawn / Getty Images)

204 Chinatown Limehouse (Stapleton Historical Collection / Heritage Images)

228 Sultan's Elephant at Picadilly Circus (Ed Liu)

all other images CJ Lim / Studio 8 Architects

CH00536290

7 Words
on Marriage

Fr Ivano Millico

All booklets are published
thanks to the generosity of the supporters
of the Catholic Truth Society

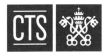

Introduction

The most beautiful thing God has created

Seven Words about *your* marriage

"Marriage is the most beautiful thing God has created".
Pope Francis pronounced these words on 1st October
2016 while on an official visit to Georgia. Virtually the
whole Catholic population – less than one per cent –
had gathered in the Church of the Assumption of
Our Lady in Tbilisi to dialogue with the Holy Father.
Amongst them a married couple raised a question,
asking for help: is it possible to believe in marriage?
Can we *still* have faith in marriage?

What follows are '*seven words*' on marriage, *your*
marriage, in seven chapters. They are mainly words
pronounced on your wedding day, taken from the
Rite of Marriage; words found on the lips of married
couples in the Bible; words of poetry and drama; words of
advice from priests, Popes and even Saints!

These words are yours – they belong to your marriage,
they are your heritage. They are meant for couples
engaged to be married as well as for married couples;
full of joy or going through difficulties and serious
problems; broken couples whose marriage has failed
them and couples too afraid or disenchanted to marry.
These words are for you, they come from the Church
who loves you and announces to you that marriage is
the most beautiful thing God has created.

Father Ivano

The bridegroom says:

> *I take Thee* to be my wedded wife
> to have and to hold from this day forward,
> for better, for worse,
> for richer, for poorer,
> in sickness and in health,
> to love and to cherish
> till death do us part.

The bride says:

> *I take Thee* to be my wedded husband
> to have and to hold from this day forward,
> for better, for worse,
> for richer, for poorer,
> in sickness and in health,
> to love and to cherish
> till death do us part.

I.

I take Thee

"Never without the Other"

At the centre of every marriage are these words: "*I take Thee*". What do they mean? In the Latin Rite of Marriage, the expression used for '*I take*' is '*accipio*'. The Latin verb '*accipere*' means much more than '*to take*', it means: '*to receive*', '*to welcome*'. When a man and a woman get married, one does not '*take*' the other, but '*receives*' another. The '*DNA*' of marriage is a *DNA* of welcoming, openness and communion.

The *DNA* of marriage

"I *take* Thee" means 'I *welcome* Thee'. Pope Francis notes:

> When we hear this word, we immediately think of something to do. But in reality welcoming is a more profound disposition: it requires not only making room for someone, but being a welcoming, available person, accustomed to giving oneself to others. As God does for us, so we do for others. Welcoming means putting things into perspective, setting right my way of thinking, understanding that life is not my private property and that time does not belong to me. It is a gradual parting

from all that is mine: my time, my rest, my rights, my plans, my agenda. One who welcomes gives up the '*me*' and allows '*you*' and '*us*' to enter his life." [1]

To marry is to 'receive' another person as he is, as she is, into your own life. It is not about trying to change that person to fit into your ideas or to suit you according to your expectations – but it is about loving *that* person, to say 'yes' to that person. In this sense, marriage is a real personal transformation from '*me*' to '*you*' and '*us*', where one spouse 'dies' to himself (herself) to find himself (herself) 'risen' in the other spouse. In marriage each one ceases to be an individual and becomes a person, that is, a sincere and definite gift of oneself to another. In fact marriage proves to be "the most effective antidote to unbridled individualism".[2] And all of this is possible because at the centre of Christian marriage is the person of Jesus Christ, the loving gift of himself.

Egolatry

Our air, our 'human environment' is corrupted by a real form of 'pollution' that corrodes souls and confounds minds and hearts, producing false illusions. This pollution is not mere selfishness or the old

---

[1]   Pope Francis, Address to the Vincentian Family on the Fourth Centenary of the Charism, St Peter's Square, 14th October 2017.

[2]   Pope Francis, Video Message to the Participants of the Third International Symposium on the Apostolic Exhortation *Amoris Laetitia* convoked by the Italian Episcopal Conference's Office for the Pastoral Care of Families.

narcissism, it is much more: it is a real form of *egolatry*. Addressing the Pontifical Academy for Life, Pope Francis spoke, as no one else before him, about this sickening and polluting air we breathe every day:

> Human beings seem now to find themselves at a special juncture in their history, in unchartered territory, as they deal with questions both old and new regarding the meaning of human life, its origin and destiny.
>
> The key feature of this moment is, in a word, the rapid spread of a culture obsessively centred on the mastery of human beings – individually and as a species – over reality. Some have even spoken of an *egolatry*, a worship of the self, on whose altar everything is sacrificed, even the most cherished human affections. This approach is far from harmless, for it induces people to gaze constantly in the mirror, to the point of being unable to turn their eyes away from themselves and towards others and the larger world. The spread of this approach has extremely grave effects on every affection and relationship in life.[3]

Christian marriage, the covenant between man and woman in marriage and family, not only is the antidote against this pollution but the place where

---

3   Pope Francis, Address to the General Assembly of The Pontifical Academy For Life, 5th October 2017.

the real meaning of being man and woman can be preserved. This meaning is connected with the capacity for communion of man "who is not just something, but someone. He is capable of self-knowledge, of self-possession and of freely giving himself and entering into communion with other persons".[4] This 'capacity' is part of the grace of the Sacrament of Marriage: to make space for another and welcome this person into my life.

Mysticism of the encounter

Marriage is a mystical experience, yes! Pope Francis has spoken of a real "*mysticism of the encounter*" which entails the ability to listen to the other and live with the other, recognising the family as the fundamental place where we come to discover who we are by encountering the "other from me".[5]

Two Catholic priests who have had a strong influence on the theological reflection of Pope Francis have written on this "mysticism of the encounter". The theologian Romano Guardini (1885-1968) in one of his texts on true *goodness* described how "from this imprisonment within myself I am free only if I find

---

[4]   *Catechism of the Catholic Church* §357; cf. Pope Francis, Encyclical Letter *Laudato Si'* §65.

[5]   Pope Francis, Apostolic Letter to all Consecrated People, 21st November 2014; See, Address to the Participants of the Conference (RE) THINKING EUROPE, Commission of the Bishops' Conferences of the European Community, 28th October 2017.

a point other from my own ego; a point above myself".[6]
The Jesuit historian Michel de Certeau (1925-1986)
developed the philosophical truth "not without the
other" – whereby every human experience begins with
the encounter with the "other from me" – into the
Christian personal truth "never without *you*".[7] Rather
than through a personal effort, our encounter with God
happens within a space where I encounter the "other
from me".

The words "I *take* Thee" pronounced in marriage echo
a very ancient Christian prayer pronounced in a low
voice by the priest before receiving Holy Communion:[8]
*I take you…I receive you…I welcome you…may I never be
parted from you…*

---

[6] Romano Guardini, *Coscienza*, Brescia, 1933.

[7] Michel de Certeau, *La Fable Mystique*, XVI-XVII siècle, Gallimard, Paris,
     1982; *La Faiblesse de Croire*, Texte établi et présenté par Luce Giard, Seuil,
     Paris 1987.

[8] From the Latin Roman Missal, prayer of the celebrant before Holy
     Communion: *Dómine Iesu Christe, Fili Dei vivi, qui ex voluntáte Patris,
     cooperánte Spíritu Sancto, per mortem tuam mundum vivificásti: líbera me per
     hoc sacrosánctum Corpus et Sánguinem tuum ab ómnibus iniquitátibus meis,
     et univérsis malis: et fac me tuis semper inhærére mandátis, et a te numquam
     separári permíttas.*

2.

She has been given to you *from* Heaven

"Accompaniment, Discernment and Providence"

Where does your husband come from? Where does your wife-to-be come from? Heaven! Yes indeed, from heaven.

Often, I find myself as a priest hearing confessions, repeating this fundamental truth about marriage over and over again: "*it is Heaven that has decided*" (*Tb* 7:12).

Accompaniment

The Bible is full of stories of families and married couples. Among them, one stands out. The Book of Tobit, a second century BC work, tells the story of Tobias and Sarah. The two will eventually fall in love and get married, but to begin with, live afar from each other, do not even know each other, and are both going through a time of darkness and great sorrow. Tobias is the only son of Tobit and Anna, a devout Jewish family who during the difficult days of the Babylonian exile keep doing good works. Yet, a series of misfortunes befalls them, bringing this upright family into destitution, and forcing the young Tobias to travel to Media in the hope of regaining some money. There lives Sarah, an only daughter,

12

whose drama evolves around her attempts at marriage. Seven times she had married, and each time, on the wedding night, her husband-to-be has died before having consummated the marriage, through the intervention of a terrible demon.

Tobias and Sarah are living two parallel situations at the limits of despair – having lost all hope, feeling utterly abandoned, ready to prefer death to life. Out of their "existential underworld of suffering" – as Pope Francis has called it[9] – comes a prayer of lament and the answer of God who sends the Archangel Raphael who unknowingly becomes Tobias's travelling companion. The rest of the Book tells how along the journey Raphael – meaning 'God's healing' – instructs Tobias on how to fight the demon, leads him to Sarah's house, helps him to overcome his fears and even arranges their wedding!

The central core of the whole Book is all about Tobias's journey from Nineveh to Ecbatana. This is not a literary technique or an interlude between a sad opening and the happy ending. No; the journey is in fact a precious time when God is at work and his plan of love slowly unfolds. Tobias is on his way to the region of Media simply to collect money deposited there and now necessary for his destitute family. In his mind, there is no other reason, no other plan. And yet, slowly, slowly, along the journey Raphael

---

9   Pope Francis, Daily Meditation, *Domus Sanctae Marthae*, 5th June 2013.

begins a dialogue with Tobias, inviting him to open his heart to a different plan, a greater plan, God's plan. On the lips of this Angel we find words like "*listen, brother*" (*Tb* 6:12, 13, 16), "*I promise you*" (*Tb* 6:13, 16). And so, along the journey Tobias becomes obedient, grows into becoming a disciple, following the angel he is initiated into the will of God so to embrace it with all his freedom.

The mission of this "good angel" (*Tb* 5:22), as a distinctive character of the Book, is to reveal the divine loving plan of God for this man and this woman, and to help them to enter into God's plan. At the outset of his journey Tobias will find this angel "ready", "standing facing him" (*Tb* 5:4), which literally means 'ahead of him'. What it means is that the plan of God is ahead of this couple, and the work of this good angel is to 'catechise' the couple, making them grow in faith and so help them respond to the plan of God for their lives.

Discernment

This beautiful biblical story carries a real theology of marriage, captured in two expressions, one by the same Raphael and the other by Sarah's father, Raguel. Familiar with Sarah's drama Tobias is afraid of even considering marrying her: "I do not wish to die", he says (*Tb* 6:15). In face of this fear of death, the Angel replies: "Do not be afraid: *she was destined to you from eternity*, and you will save her. She will follow you, and I promise my word she will give you children" (*Tb* 6:18). The Angel is announcing to Tobias the 'plan of God' for his life, a plan of life not of death, a plan of love and salvation. "And when Tobias heard Raphael say this...he fell so deeply in love with her that he could no longer call his heart his own" (*Tb* 6:19). Is Tobias falling in love with a girl he has never seen before? A girl renowned for her cursed past marriages? A girl whose marital bed is simply a grave? No. Tobias has been initiated by the Angel – image of the Church who accompanies engaged couples and married couples along their journey – into the will of God for his life. Listening to the Angel, Tobias is enlightened, and so 'falls deeply in love' with this plan of God. Thanks to the words and the advice of the Angel this young man has learned to pass from fear to trust and enter into God's plan deeply, with his whole self. Man discerns and consents to the divine plan, discovers, accepts and wants what God wants, and so finds in this consent, even before the fulfilment of the actual plan of God, rest and deep joy.

The other expression which speaks of God's plan for marriage is found on the lips of Sarah's father, Raguel. He is the one who presides over the wedding (cf. *Tb* 7). Before entrusting his only daughter to Tobias as his wife and sitting down at the wedding banquet, Raguel reveals not only the truth about her past failed marriages, but the deeper truth about this wedding: "*It is heaven that has decided she shall be yours... So, receive her...she is given to you from today for ever*" (*Tb* 7:12). Fully conscious of the death threatening them, Raguel announces: "the Lord will provide for you" (*Tb* 7:11), a Hebrew expression which means 'the Lord will act with you...will intervene in your histories...will lead your lives'.

What the Book of Tobit is telling us is that it is only on the strength of these words that the wedding is celebrated and Tobias and Sarah get married. Without the Angel Raphael and without Raguel there would be no marriage! These two characters represent 'the Church' – Raphael, the voice of the catechist-travelling companion, and Raguel, the voice of the father-priest. Marriage is the fruit of a loving encounter, yes, but also the fruit of a spiritual accompaniment because it is a vocation. Pope Francis addressing the Salesians, experts on the pedagogy of vocation, warns them: "the vocational geography has changed and is changing and this means a new demanding formation where *accompaniment* and *discernment* are needed."[10] *Accompaniment* and *discernment* are nothing else but Raphael and Raguel in the "vocational geography" of the story of Tobias and Sarah.

---

[10] Pope Francis, Address to the Participants in the General Chapter of the Salesians, 31st March 2014.

Providence

It is Heaven that has decided she shall be yours... (cf. *Tb* 7:12). It is *not* Tobias who has chosen Sarah first, it is not him who wants her first; God has chosen for him. The Book of Tobit is really important, because here, marriage is really a sacrament, the sign of a presence, the living presence of God who realises a plan of love and salvation. Out of this marriage that was destined only for death comes life and healing, for the couple and far beyond them. Marriage is not a private affair; before being the fruit of a personal choice by man and woman, it is willed by God for the joy of the spouses and for the healing of the people around them.[11]

According to Jewish tradition – and our Christian faith – every marriage celebrated on earth has been 'made' in heaven. There is no union between spouses not wanted by God. Every match responds to a divine will, to a precise divine plan even when it looks completely random or fortuitous, especially the meeting between man and woman. In marriage a mystery is realised: before a man chooses his wife, before a woman chooses her husband, someone else has already chosen for them. Their choice is but obedience to a divine will, a free response to the secret action of God who helps us to fulfil the design he has prepared for us from all eternity. How beautiful it is, and how comforting it is to know

---

[11] See the beautiful commentary on the Book of Tobit by Divio Barsotti, *Meditazione sul Libro di Tobia*, Queriniana, Brescia, 1969.

that greater than any of our wills, and more ancient than any of our thoughts, is the will of God for us (for you)!

When you look at your wife's face, when you see your husband, you are in front of the love of God for you. He 'comes' from heaven...she 'comes' from heaven... from God for you. *It is Heaven that has decided...*

Yes, heaven has decided, but have you met Raphael and Raguel? Do you know who they are in your "vocational geography"? Do you have catechists, a spiritual director, or an older married couple helping you in your steps towards marriage and after?

Before every couple gets married they need to be accompanied and helped in their discernment. Once married, this journey needs to continue. They need Raphael and Raguel, in order to hear these truths and these promises: the Lord is the *Lord* of their histories; he is the one who has brought their lives together; he will provide for them, healing their sufferings and transforming sorrow into blessings.

This detail of the painting of Filippo Lippi shows hand in hand not Tobias and Sarah, but Tobias and the Archangel Raphael. Earth and heaven are hand in hand: heaven is leading this young man to meet his wife-to-be. They are together, they are walking together, but heaven is ahead, heaven has decided, and man slowly and freely discerns, enters the plan of God and discovers the providence of God.

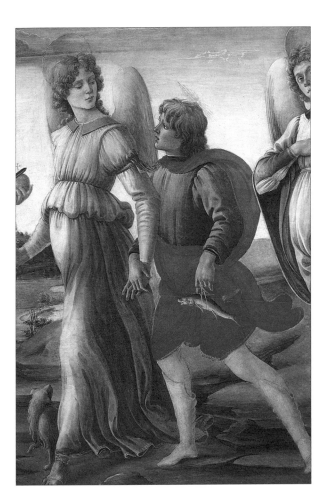

3.
Argue as much as you want...but forgive

"Forgive me – the vocation and
the mission of the Christian family"

When a couple gets married everyone tries to give them some advice and good tips. In this third chapter, this 'third word' on marriage, is in fact advice from the Church. "I", confessed Pope Francis, "always give this advice to newly wedded couples":

> Argue as much as you like. If the plates fly, let them! But never end the day without making peace! Never! And if married people learn to say: "forgive me, I was tired", or even a little gesture, this is peace. Then carry on with life the next day. This is a beautiful secret.[12]

Three essential words!

When the Church speaks of the Sacrament of Marriage, she is very well aware of the frailty of the human condition and of the many difficulties two spouses experience: work, money, children. Sacrament simply

---

[12] Pope Francis, Meeting with the Clergy, Consecrated People and Members of Diocesan Pastoral Councils, Cathedral of San Rufino, Assisi, 4th October 2013.

means that there is a 'bond' with God and this is at the root of the marital bond between husband and wife. Christ is in the 'middle' of the married couple and says to him 'forgive her', and says to her 'forgive him'!

> There is always arguing in marriage, sometimes the plates even fly. Yet we must not become saddened by this, this is the human condition. The secret is that love is stronger than the moment when there is arguing, and therefore I always advise spouses: do not let a day when you have argued end without making peace. Always! And to make peace it isn't necessary to call the United Nations to come to the house and make peace. A little gesture is sufficient, a caress, and then let it be! Until tomorrow! And tomorrow begin again. And this is life, carrying on, carrying on with courage and the desire to live together. And this is truly great, it is beautiful! Married life is such a beautiful thing and we must treasure it always, treasure the children. On other occasions in this Square I have mentioned something else which is so helpful for marriage. There are three words that always need to be said, three words that need to be said at home: *Please, Thank you,* and *Forgive me.*[13]

Often Pope Francis has spoken of a particular '*style*' of married life. Living together as husband and wife is a form of '*art*' which demands learning three words:

---

[13] Pope Francis, General Audience, 2nd April 2014.

Please, Thank you, Forgive me. Three essential words! We say please so as not to be forceful in family life: "*May I please do this? Would you be happy if I did this?*" We do this with a language that seeks agreement. We say thank you, thank you for love! But be honest with me, how many times do you say thank you to your wife, and you to your husband? How many days go by without uttering this word, thanks! And the last word: sorry. We all make mistakes and on occasion someone gets offended in the marriage, in the family, and sometimes – I say – plates are smashed, harsh words are spoken but please listen to my advice: don't ever let the sun set without reconciling. Peace is made each day in the family: "*Please forgive me*", and then you start over. Please, thank you, sorry! Let us say these words in our families![14]

Who pays the divorce fees?

It is normal, completely normal, to argue and fight. In Tbilisi, Pope Francis spoke to a married couple who in front of misunderstanding and problems in their marriage were faced with the temptation to divorce: "Well...let's solve this through divorce, so I can find another man, and he can find another woman, and we can start again". "Do you know", asked Pope Francis

---

[14] Pope Francis, Address to the Participants in the Pilgrimage of Families During the Year of Faith, St Peter's Square, 26th October 2013.

then, "who pays the divorce fees? Two people pay", said the Pope. "But who are they? Who pays?" asked the Pope:

Both of them [husband and wife] pay? Yes, but more… God pays, because when 'one flesh' is divided, the image of God is soiled. And the children pay. You do not know, dear brothers and sisters, you do not know how much children suffer, the little ones, when they witness the arguments and the separation of parents! Everything should be done to save a marriage. But is it normal to have arguments in marriage? Yes, it is normal. It happens. Sometimes 'plates fly'. But if love is real, then peace is made quickly. I offer this advice to spouses: argue as much as you want, but don't let the day end without making peace. Do you know why? Because 'the cold war' of the day after is extremely dangerous. How many marriages are saved when they have the courage at the end of the day to not make speeches but rather offer a caress, and peace is made! It is true, there are more complex situations, when the devil gets involved and entices the man with another woman who seems more beautiful than his wife, or when the devil entices the woman with another man who seems better than her husband. Ask for help straightaway. When this temptation comes, ask for help immediately. [15]

---

[15] Pope Francis, Meeting with Priests, Religious, Seminarians and Pastoral Workers, Church of the Assumption of the Blessed Virgin Mary, Tbilisi, Georgia, 1st October 2016.

The capacity to forgive

The capacity to forgive is in being forgiven first. "Love forgives all", wrote St Paul in his famous lyrical hymn to love (cf. *1 Co* 13:4-7), so much used at weddings – but first we need to be loved in being forgiven. Looking at the original Greek phrase used by Paul we read that love "takes no account of evil", "it is not resentful" (*1 Co* 13:5). The opposite of resentment is forgiveness, which is rooted in a positive attitude that seeks to understand other people's weaknesses to the point of excusing them.[16]

In a beautiful catechesis on the family Pope Francis spoke of the "treasure of mutual forgiveness" as the vocation and mission of the family – the 'salt' that gives flavour and hope to the people we meet every day, and the 'leaven' of a culture of encounter:

> The family is a great *training ground for the mutual giving and forgiving* without which no love can last for long. Without self-giving and seeking forgiveness love does not last, it does not endure. One cannot live without seeking forgiveness, or at least, one cannot live at peace, especially in the family. We wrong one another every day. We must take into account these mistakes, due to our frailty and our selfishness. There is a *simple secret* to healing wounds and avoiding recriminations. It is this: *do not let the day end without*

---

[16] Pope Francis, Apostolic Exhortation *Amoris Laetitia*, §105.

apologising, without making peace between husband and wife... If we learn to apologise promptly and to give each other mutual forgiveness, the wounds heal, the marriage grows stronger, and the family becomes an increasingly stronger home.

If we learn to live this way in the family, we can also do so outside, wherever we may be... *The capacity to forgive and to seek forgiveness is part of the vocation and the mission of the family*. Practising forgiveness not only saves families from divisiveness but makes them capable of helping society to be less heartless and less cruel. Yes, each act of forgiveness fixes the cracks in the house and strengthens its walls... Conversely, we may even make beautiful sermons, and perhaps drive away some demons, but in the end the Lord will not recognise us as his disciples, because we did not have the capacity to forgive and ask others to forgive us![17]

Prayers of forgiveness

To be married and to stay married is a real challenge. This is why prayer is a necessity of married life. But which prayer? What kind of prayers? Here many couples get discouraged and feel spiritually inadequate. I would simply suggest to every married

---

[17] Pope Francis, General Audience, 4th November 2015. See also Video Message to the Participants of the Third International Symposium on the Apostolic Exhortation *Amoris Laetitia*.

couple to recite together every night before going to bed the prayer of the *Our Father*. In this prayer you say: "*Forgive us our trespasses, as we forgive those who trespass against us*". Yes, every day, every night, pray these words and ask forgiveness.

> It is easy to be sceptical about this. Many people – even Christians – think it is an exaggeration. It is said: yes, they are fine words, but it is impossible to put them into practice. But thanks be to God it is not so. Indeed, it is precisely in receiving forgiveness from God that we in turn are capable of forgiving others.[18]

This is why husband and wife need to listen to another voice, not the one of their spouse, but a voice external to them. This is the voice of the Church who announces the mercy of God, the love of God for sinners. For us Catholics this beautiful voice is heard in the Sacrament of Confession where we are forgiven, freely and always, and receive the grace to forgive others. When we sinners hear this voice spoken to us, we learn to move from 'being forgiven' to 'being forgiving'.

> Let us learn to acknowledge our mistakes and to ask for forgiveness. "Forgive me if today I raised my voice"; "I'm sorry if I passed without greeting you";

---

[18] Pope Francis, General Audience, 4th November 2015. See also Video Message to the Participants of the Third International Symposium on the Apostolic Exhortation *Amoris Laetitia*.

"excuse me if I was late", "if this week I was very silent", "if I spoke too much without ever listening"; "excuse me if I forgot"; "I'm sorry I was angry and I took it out on you"... We can say many "I'm sorrys" every day. We all know that the perfect family does not exist, nor a perfect husband or wife... We sinners exist.[19]

There is another experience of prayer we all need in order to forgive others: forgiving ourselves. Sometimes to hear the words '*you are forgiven*' is not enough; we need to '*forgive ourselves*'. Often at the root of our lack of forgiveness towards others are wounds of our past history and the incapacity to accept ourselves as we are with our own limitations, defects, and many imperfections. In prayer, especially silent prayer of adoration, we are exposed to our true selves and at the same time to the unconditional love of God for us as we are with no merits on our part. We receive the grace to forgive ourselves, in order to have the same attitude towards others.[20]

Do not end the day at war!

"Be angry, but do not sin; do not let the sun go down on your anger" (*Ep* 4:26).

---

[19] Pope Francis, Address to Engaged Couples Preparing for Marriage, 14th February 2014.

[20] Pope Francis, Apostolic Exhortation *Amoris Laetitia*, §§107-108.

4.
What God has united,
let no man put asunder

"The bridal chamber"

In the celebration of marriage immediately after the bride and the bridegroom, while joining their hands, have openly expressed their will to be married, the priest says these words: *"What God joins together, let no one put asunder"*. What is the meaning of these words?

The prayer of Tobias and Sarah

In chapter eight of the Book of Tobit we find the prayer Tobias and Sarah, newly wedded, recite in their bridal chamber at the evening of their marriage. The young Tobias is deeply in love with Sarah. In fact in the previous chapter of the Book we read that he is so much in love with Sarah that he could no longer call his heart his own! What a beautiful scene! How beautiful it is to see a man and woman in love, how refreshing, how attractive is love. They are a young couple, they desire one another, they want to be with each other, they love one another. But they have discovered something very important: there is something they cannot do by themselves. There is something their deep love for one another cannot do. They cannot become one.

They cannot unite each other and become one body. They can't. Only God unites. This is his proper character: to unite. And so, on the evening of their marriage, before they come together in love and become one body, they need to pray.

Tobias rose from the bed, and said to Sarah,
    "Get up, my sister!
You and I must pray and petition the Lord to win
    his grace and his mercy."
She stood up, and they began praying for protection,
    this is how he began:

"You are blessed, O God of our fathers;
blessed, too, is your name for ever and ever.
Let the heavens bless you
and all things you have made for evermore.
It was you who created Adam,
you who created Eve his wife to be his help and support;
and from these two the human race was born.
It was you who said, 'It is not good that the man should
    be alone;
let us make him a helpmate like himself.'
And so I do not take my sister for any lustful motive;
I do it in singleness of heart.
Be kind enough to have pity on her and on me
and bring us to old age together."

And together they said, "Amen, Amen"
and lay down for the night.
(*Tb* 8:4-9)

Before laying down in bed for the night, before coming together in deep intimacy, this married couple prayed. Each one of them 'stands up' and 'rises up' from the nuptial bed. It looks like a description of the Jewish traditional way of praying by standing up, but its meaning is greater. It means that before a married couple can enter into relationship with one another, each of them needs to enter into relationship with God.

Before uttering words, the prayer of Tobias and Sarah is a simple physical action, a change of body posture: *up!* From turning to each other, to turning upwards to God! To pray is not simply to recite prayers. To pray is to change the position of our body, it is to turn up to God, to become a 'vertical' body, turned firstly towards heaven. Before the bodies of Tobias and Sarah can enter into love and become one body, they need to stand up and turn to God.

Why? Because only God can unite their bodies, only God can unite the bodies of man and woman in marriage and make of them one body. The relationship between the two of them, the most intimate relationship, demands another presence, because no union amongst man and woman can happen outside of God.

By praying Tobias and Sarah take the anchor of their marriage and throw it up to heaven…and with their *Amen* make sure it is firmly hooked! Because their union depends on God. Their marriage depends on God. Your marriage depends on God!

"What God has joined together, let no man put asunder" (*Mt* 19:6). Jesus pronounces these words in the course of a confrontation with the Pharisees about marriage and the possibility of divorce. "What *God* has united". These words are the anchor of every Christian marriage, because they mean that the ultimate and prime guarantee of every Christian marriage is to be found in the action of God. It would be terrible to say instead "What *man* has united, let no man separate". To say this is to say that your marriage depends on you, relies on your strength, on your constancy and work, but this is not true. Christ knows far too well the heart of man to say these words. He knows, as you know (!), that the promises of a man and a woman deeply in love with each other are a fragile foundation of their married life. Yes, of course, their love is real and beautiful, but it has to become a vertical love, a love hooked into heaven, anchored unto God's love.[21]

The prayer of Tobias and Sarah tells us how to look for this love of God. Their prayer is how to search for this treasure which is the promise of God to the newly married couple. Married life has to be a life of prayer. This is the teaching of Tobias and Sarah. God is not a stranger to your marriage, an interloper, an alien presence, a sort of necessary but unwanted visitor, No! It is him who creates intimacy and grants protection.

---

[21] See "Una Sola Carne, en un Mismo Espíritu: Teología del Matrimonio", by José Granados, 2014.

Tobias and Sarah conclude their prayer saying together "*Amen, Amen*". In a Christian marriage there is also the *Amen* of God: God commits himself to the married couple, he unites them, he is the guarantor of their unity. Behind the promises of the bride and the bridegroom, behind every promise man and woman can pronounce, there is a promise received, the promise of God, the *Amen* of God.

Liturgy of healing

As we have seen above, in chapter eight of the Book of Tobit the Bible enters inside the bridal room of a newly wedded couple and tells the spouses what to do: to pray!

We need to recall some facts which are in the background. Sarah had been given in marriage seven times and each time, before coming together with her bridegroom, each one had died in the bridal room because of the action of an evil spirit that killed them. This evil spirit Asmodeus is the worst of all demons (cf. *Tb* 3:8, 17; 6:8, 14-15, 16, 17; 8:3; 12:14). Jewish writings and rabbinic commentaries, dating around the same time as the Book of Tobit, associate this demon – enemy of the conjugal union – with lustful passions. The young Tobias fears a similar death, and as the couple are inside the bedroom, Sarah's father and his servants are secretly digging a grave in the back garden ready to bury Tobias without anyone knowing it.

All of this may sound like folklore or legends, yet it is definitively true that when a married couple enter their bedroom to celebrate love they carry with themselves their own sexual histories which can violate conjugal love.

It is natural for husband and wife to make themselves attractive and beautiful for each other. God has created sexual attraction and desire, but husband and wife can hurt each other by making love not for the good of the other but for self-gratification. Sexual love in marriage can turn inwards and instead of being the expression of a self-gift it can become 'lustful' – that is, possessive and selfish. This may be due to past histories marked by pornography carrying false sexual projections or expectations; fears and wounds due to sins caused or suffered; distortions due to an improper understandings of sexuality, being over-scrupulous or too loose. Sometimes it can even carry the consequences of deep traumas. Thus inside the 'sexual baggage' of a married couple could enter a destructive demon threatening their joyful sexual union. How can the sexual union in marriage become a real place of healing and restoration?

Between September 1979 and November 1984 Pope St John Paul II devoted his Wednesday general audiences to presenting an in-depth biblical explanation of the Sacrament of Marriage and human sexuality; in total one hundred and thirty-eight catecheses that came to be known as the 'Theology of the Body'. Commenting on the wedding night in the Book of Tobit,[22]

---

[22] Pope John Paul II, General Audience, 27th June 1984.

John Paul II spoke of the struggle between the forces of evil and the forces of good that go on while husband and wife are becoming one. The sexual act between the newly wedded Tobias and Sarah – and indeed every married couple – presents itself as a real battleground between death and life. In this combat the malefic action of the interloper Asmodeus is contrasted by the salvific advice of the messenger of God, the Archangel Raphael (cf. *Tb* 7:16-18). What the narrator of the Book is telling us about the Sacrament of Marriage is that in the bridal room we find not only husband and wife, but also evil and good, demons and angels, and in the middle of all of them we find a 'fish'. Yes, a fish! Going a few chapters back in the Book, at the beginning of his journey towards Media, Tobias had had a close encounter with a big fish that came out from the water (cf. *Tb* 6:2-6). This fish could be seen as a symbol of Jesus Christ.[23] Listening to the advice of his companion Tobias wrestled with this big fish, grasped it, and cut out its heart, gall and liver and kept them as healing remedies:

> Then [continued Raphael] once you are in the bridal room, take the heart and liver of the fish and lay a little of it on the burning incense. The reek will rise, the demon will smell it and flee, and there is no danger that he will ever be found near the girl again. Then, before you sleep together, first stand up, both of you, and pray. Ask the Lord of heaven to grant you his grace and protection. Do not be afraid. (*Tb* 6:17-18)

As Tobias and Sarah enter their bedroom on their wedding night they are both aware of the battle that goes on inside of their marriage – between loving the other and using the other, between giving and possessing, between fear and trust – so remembering Raphael's advice instead of a poetic romantic duet or a dialogue between the newlyweds, the reality of the battle quietens their loving dialogue and what emerges is another dimension of love, a 'liturgical' dimension. On their wedding night, Tobias and Sarah speak one single voice, that is a voice of prayer, their 'body language' becomes the language of a liturgy proper to their sacrament.[24]

The liturgy celebrated by Tobias and Sarah (cf. *Tb* 8:1-8) which will bring them together in the sexual act is made of three parts. The first part (vv. 1-3) is a prayer of deliverance, a form of exorcism, when the sexual act is set free from the demon of lust. The second part of the liturgy is a real profession of faith, a sort of 'nuptial creed', when the couple turns to God in trust recounting their histories of salvation (vv. 4-6). The third part of the prayer is an 'epicletic' prayer when the couple, now healed, call down in faith the Holy Spirit as they become one (vv. 7-8).

Let us look at these parts in detail.

---

[23] Amongst the earliest references to Jesus Christ is the image of a fish, *ichthus* in Greek, acrostic for Jesus Christ Son of God Saviour.

[24] Pope John Paul II, General Audience, 27th June 1984.

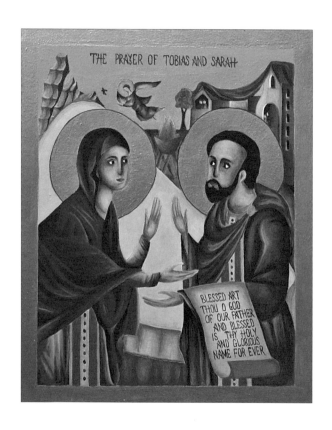

THE PRAYER OF TOBIAS AND SARAH

BLESSED ART
THOU O GOD
OF OUR FATHER
AND BLESSED
IS THY HOLY
AND GLORIOUS
NAME FOR EVER

Deliverance

The beautiful icon here beside shows these three moments. In the middle, between husband and wife – Tobias and Sarah – is a burning brazier where the heart and the liver of the fish are burning. The burning 'heart' and 'liver' of the fish are symbols of the burning love of Christ for us, his Passion and bitter suffering on the cross where life and death in mighty battle saw Christ victorious. Behind the burning fire we see an angel, the Archangel Raphael, casting away a little black demon, sending him away into the desert not to harm the couple any more.

> Tobias remembered Raphael's advice; he went to his bag, took the fish's heart and liver out of it, and put some on the burning incense. The reek of the fish distressed the demon, who fled through the air to Egypt. Raphael pursued him there, shackled him and strangled him forthwith. (vv. 2-3)

In the Name of Jesus Christ, in his presence, the married couple makes a personal renunciation to the demon of lust who threatens their relationship; renounces the spirit of sexual possession and manipulation; desire for control and fantasies; seeking interior and exterior freedom. In the Name of Jesus Christ, the demon that was keeping siege around their nuptial bed, the demon who was binding them in fear, is thus cast away not to return again.

Of this healing action Pope Benedict XVI wrote:

> Raphael heals the disturbed communion between man and woman. He heals their love. He drives out the demons who over and over again exhaust and destroy their love. He purifies the atmosphere between the two and gives them the ability to accept each other for ever. In Tobit's account this healing is recounted with legendary images. In the New Testament, the order of marriage established in creation and threatened in many ways by sin, is healed through Christ's acceptance of it in his redeeming love. He makes marriage a sacrament: his love, put on a cross for us, is the healing power which in all forms of chaos offers the capacity for reconciliation, purifies the atmosphere, mends the wounds.[25]

Profession of faith

The second part of this liturgy is a call to prayer – "you and I must pray" (*Tb* 8:4). Leaning on Tobias's arm is a scroll, the text of their prayer, a profession of faith:

> You are blessed, O God of our fathers,
> and blessed is your holy and glorious name for ever.
> Let the heavens bless you
> and all things you have made for evermore.

---

[25] Pope Benedict XVI, Mass of the Three Archangels, St Peter's Basilica, 29th September 2007.

It was you who created Adam,
you who created Eve his wife to be his help and
    support;
and from these two the human race was born.
It was you who said, "It is not good that the man
    should be alone;
let us make him a helpmate like himself."
(vv. 4-6)

This prayer echoes the faith of Tobias and Sarah in God the Creator and God the author of history – beginning with Adam and Eve – who has a plan for their human love that is a call, the vocation to become one in marriage, and make the glory of God appear. Pope John Paul II commenting on this text has described it as a "spousal creed", the spinal column on which spouses can lean as they respond to the calling of God.

Holy Spirit

The third part of the liturgy is we can say an 'epiclesis'. The Holy Spirit, the spirit of God, can now come down and enter the temple of this marriage and rest in it:

And now I do not take my sister for any lustful motive;
I do it in singleness of heart.
Be kind enough to have mercy on her and on me
    and bring us to old age together.
And together they said, "Amen, Amen".
(vv. 7-8)

The nuptial night is above all the moment when the spouses become one. This union is threatened by an evil 'spirit' which disturbs, destroys communion, and makes it impossible for husband and wife to be one. This spirit is stronger than them, they need the 'fish', they need Christ. Healed by the 'fish', in faith, Tobias and Sarah receive a new 'spirit' which is a spirit of communion which brings life and fruits.

Your bedroom, the nuptial bedroom, is not just another room in your house. It is a sacred space, it is the room where you celebrate the Sacrament of Marriage. It is the room where you say *Amen* to each other and where God says *Amen* to you.

The Palazzo Ducale in Mantua, home to the Gonzaga family, is covered by frescoes of the renaissance artist Andrea Mantegna. His best surviving work is '*La Camera degli Sposi*' – the bridal chamber – where the decoration consists of a painted dome-like 'lookout' on the ceiling. The overall scene gives to the viewer the illusion of looking up to heaven, while angels are looking down. This *trompe l'oeil* is not only a masterpiece work of art in perspective but it also has a theological character. Its purpose is to give to the room a third dimension, 'opening up' to heaven the ceiling of the bridal chamber. The nuptial bedroom is not made of four closed walls; it is a room open up to heaven, where heaven is present, where the Holy Spirit can come down.

It is normal to have a crucifix in your bedroom, or an icon. I remember over my parents' nuptial bed a tapestry woven by my mother representing the face of Christ. I know of wives who give great care to their bed-linen and keep their nuptial bed immaculate, not being fussy but because it reveals the holiness and peace of the room. Another physical sign used to signify the presence of God over the nuptial bed is the baldacchino, a ceremonial canopy made of stone or precious fabric placed over an altar or a throne. Inside many churches you can find marble pillars holding a baldachin over the main altar. The origins of this feature are in the Bible where the presence of God – *Shekinah* in Hebrew – was signified by a tent or a veil, which in a hot country like Israel would provide shade and protection. The Bible speaks of a movable "sacred tent", a "baldachin", carried by the people of God in the desert, and if you think of the procession on the feast of *Corpus Christi* still the presence of God in the Holy Eucharist is carried under a 'sacred tent'.

Your nuptial bed is a holy place where a liturgy is celebrated. A liturgy of healing, a profession of faith, and where the Spirit of God comes down as husband and wife become one body. Your bedroom has to reflect this truth of your marriage. I don't suggest you have a *trompe l'oeil* on the ceiling, or a baldachin bedroom necessarily, but married couples need to be reminded of the holiness of that space, of the 'vertical' dimension of your marriage, a real sanctuary where God wants to live and act in your married life.

5.
Receive this ring as a sign of my love and fidelity

"The Wedding Rings"

There is one thing every engaged couple definitely has to do before getting married: buy the wedding rings!

*To prepare young people for marriage,
it is necessary to teach them love*

When the young Father Karol Wojtyla received his first appointment in 1948 as curate in the small village of Niegowic, at the foothills of the Carpathian Mountains, he literally visited every house of his rural parish and began regular meetings with engaged couples and newlyweds. During his short eight months in the Church of the Assumption of Our Lady he prepared thirteen couples for the Sacrament of Marriage. When moved to the Parish of St Florian, a few-minutes' walk from Krakow's Old Town, Father Wojtyla set up an innovative marriage preparation course, the very first programme of this kind in the whole history of the Archdiocese. In those days, Catholic couples would only meet with a priest prior to their wedding to complete the necessary legal documents and discuss the details of the celebration, nothing more! What today we call marriage preparation is the inspiration of the curate Wojtyla! Over his twenty eight months he celebrated more than 160 marriages, an average of two weddings per week![26]

Forty years later, looking back at those days of ministry, the now Pope John Paul II would write in the book *Crossing the Threshold of Hope*:

> It is this vocation to love [marriage] that naturally allows us to draw close to the young. As a priest I realised this very early. I felt almost an inner call in this direction. It is necessary to prepare young people for marriage, *it is necessary to teach them love.* Love is not something that is learned, and yet there is nothing else as important to learn! As a young priest I learned to love human love. This has been one of the fundamental themes of my priesthood, my ministry in the pulpit, in the confessional, and also in my writing. If one loves human love, there naturally arises the need to commit oneself completely to the service of "beautiful love", because love is beautiful, it is beautiful.[27]

After two years in St Florian the charismatic Father Wojtyla created a group of young lay people, mostly

---

26 Yves Semen, *La Sexualité Selon Jean-Paul II*, Presses de la Renaissance, 2004. See George Weigel, *Witness to Hope*, the biography of Pope John Paul II, pp. 91-98.

27 Pope John Paul II, *Crossing the Threshold of Hope*, pp. 122-123.

engaged and married couples. In this context, Father Wojtyla, then Bishop and Cardinal, spiritually accompanied couples, exchanged with them time of relaxation and serious reflection on major questions of vocation and moral life. Pope St John Paul II would refer to these young couples as his 'formators' allowing him to know marriage from the inside. From this pastoral experience came in 1960 – when already a Bishop – a poetic drama and meditation on the Sacrament of Marriage called *The Jeweller's Shop*, as well as his first major book *Love and Responsibility* on sexual morality.[28]

Anna and Stefan

The Jeweller's Shop is a play in three acts, rotating around three different couples and their intertwined dramatic struggles with love and marriage. According to the style of the '*theatre of the word*', the play is spartan in scenography and mostly made of individual characters' interrelated monologues. Act Two reveals a marriage in an advanced stage of breakdown. Anna and Stefan are suffering from disappointment and disillusionment. The 'inner taste' of their marriage has turned bitter and "permeates everything we happen to say, think or do; it permeates even our smile". On the surface nothing seems to change, but within the soul of this marriage a rift has opened and its edges could move apart wider

---

28 Karol Wojtyla (Pope John Paul II), *Love and Responsibility*, Ignatius Press, 1981; *The Jeweller's Shop*, Ignatius Press, 1992.

and wider, at any rate, with little hope of moving closer together again. This marriage is wounded; will it heal of itself?

The question at the heart of Act Two – the question of many, many marriages – is whether love and fidelity can be reduced to feelings and emotional states, or is there a deeper foundation? Is there a 'truth' about your marriage which is bigger than your feelings?

At this point a chance interlocutor appears in the play. On her way home Anna often walked past the Old Town jeweller's shop. In the past she paid little attention to it, but since the rift in her marriage, she had begun to look at golden wedding rings as symbols of human love and marital faith now far gone...

One day, on the way back from work,
passing by the jeweller's shop,
I thought I might as well sell this ring of mine.
So this time I decided to go in.
The jeweller examined the workmanship,
   weighed the ring
for a long time in his fingers and looked into my eyes.
For a while he was reading the date of our wedding
engraved inside the ring.
Again he looked into my eyes, put the ring on the
   scales...
then said, "This ring does not weigh anything,
the needle does not move from zero
and I cannot make it show even a milligram.

Your husband must be alive –
in which case neither of your rings, taken separately,
will weigh anything – only both together will
    register.
My jeweller's scales have this peculiarity
that they weigh not the metal
but the man's entire being and fate."
Ashamed, I took the ring back
and left the shop without a word
– I think, though, that he followed me with his eyes.

A splendid meditation, but what does it mean for your marriage? Where is the healing of the broken bond between Stefan and Anna to be found? Where is the healing of your wounded marriage?

The only time a 'ring' appears in the New Testament is in the Parable of the Prodigal Son in chapter fifteen of the Gospel of Luke. A well-known story. As the repentant son returns to his father's house, hungry and poor, carrying in his body the consequences of his many sins, the father runs towards him, full of compassion, embraces him and kisses him, calls his servants saying: "Bring quickly the best robe, and put it on him; *put a ring* on his hand, and shoes to his feet, and bring the fatted calf and kill it, let us eat and celebrate for this son of mine was dead and he is back to life; he was lost, and is found" (*Lk* 15:22-14).

It is significant that in the play the decision to sell the wedding ring comes from the incapacity to forgive: "shall I forgive?" Anna asks herself. We are not told what it is that she finds impossible to forgive, but the encounter with the jeweller changes her. Entering Krakow's Old Town jeweller's shop Anna discovered that when emotions and feelings disappear, what remains is the reality of two persons who have met in marriage with the gift of each person to the other. This is the 'truth' of the wedding ring: the self-giving love of one spouse to the other, a truth which purifies the love of the couple and makes it more and more resemble the divine love of God the Father.[29]

The golden ring you wear on your finger, the wedding ring Anna wanted to sell, carries this truth. It is the sign of the love and fidelity of God the Father to each one of you, husband and wife. In many languages the wedding ring is called 'faith' or 'truth', not only the faithfulness of the spouses, but the faithfulness of God to both of you. It is the sign that *you are forgiven by God*, that you are loved as you are, that your love can be resurrected from death, and that any rift in your marriage can be crossed thanks to the love of God the Father for each one of you. This is why the wedding ring has no weight by itself, because it is not a metal jewel, it is the ring of God the Father, the ring of Our Father, it is the truth of God's love and fidelity for each one of you when your loving feelings are dead and your fidelity gone.

[29] Rocco Buttilglione, *The Thought of the Man Who Became Pope John Paul II*, 1997, p. 257.

It is good to look at your wedding ring from time to time, during the day, and remember the words you pronounced on your wedding day:

Receive this ring
as a sign of my love and fidelity
in the name of the Father, and of the Son, and of the
 Holy Spirit.

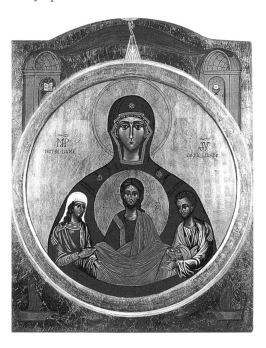

6.

Love

"Are you afraid of love?"
"Yes, I am afraid."

I cannot really conclude this short booklet on *Seven Words on Marriage* without mentioning the word "*Love*". But what does it mean to *love* your spouse?

The whole secret of love

This is the very question at the heart of Act Two of Karol Wojtyla's *The Jeweller's Shop*. Besides Anna and Stefan, and the Old Town's jeweller, there is a third mysterious character in the play called Adam – perhaps the *porte-parole* for the author himself. The dialogue between Adam and Anna takes an unexpected turn and leads into a meditation on the meaning of human love:

Is not love a matter of the senses and of a climate
    which unites and makes two people walk in the
    sphere of their feeling?
– this is the whole truth.
Adam, however, did not fully agree with this.
Love is, according to him, a synthesis of the two
    people's existence

which converges, as it were, at a certain point,
and makes them into one.

The greatest drama of human existence is, according to Adam, the incapacity to discover the whole secret of love:

> The surface of love has its current – swift, flickering, changeable. A kaleidoscope of waves and situations full of attraction. This current is sometimes so stunning that it carries people away – women and men. They get carried away by the thought they have absorbed the whole secret of love, but in fact they have not yet even touched it.

The mission of Adam, the mission of the Church, is to help married couples to discover that on the other side of all those loves that fill our lives – there is *Love!* And, to love means to give life through death...and this is when fear appears:

> [Anna] I clearly saw Stefan's face...
> I have seen the face I hate, and the face I ought to love...
> I am afraid.

> [Adam] You are afraid of love. Are you really afraid
>   of love?

> [Anna] Yes. I am afraid... That man had Stefan's face.
>   I am afraid of that face.

Anna has discovered the limit of human love – the love for the enemy. She cannot live without love and she is calling for a love she does not have. The face is the man she cannot love. She is afraid to love him, she is afraid to die for her husband.

Cana: meeting the Bridegroom

The first time the Gospels speak of a married couple – at Cana in Galilee (cf. *Jn* 2:1-12) – this same drama appears. According to Jewish tradition weddings would last seven whole days, and suddenly on the third day this married couple experiences a real human drama – "they have no wine" (*Jn* 2:3). Wine in biblical language means joy, love, blessings. There is no feast without wine, no blessing without a raised cup of wine, no joy without wine, because wine is the fruit of the Promised Land, it is the sweet fruit of God's promises to man and woman. Like Anna and Stefan, the married couple of Cana experienced the drama of human love. Love, human love, spousal love has reached its end, nothing remains!

Wojtyła's play and John's Gospel become one and the same act – Anna and Stefan become the married couple of Cana. In the middle of this drama Adam announces the hour of the coming of a mysterious bridegroom... and Mary announces the hour of Christ...

"The Bridegroom will come shortly..." says Adam to Anna.
I said this, thinking of the love which has died in her soul.
The Bridegroom passes through so many streets,
meeting so many different people.
Passing, he touches the love that is in them.

This is what happens at Cana. Wojtyla's "Bridegroom" is Jesus Christ. He asks the married couple to fill stone jars with water. In Jewish mentality there are several kinds of water, from spring water – living water – to stagnant water, like the one found in these stone jars used for the ablutions – dirty water, water lacking life.

Christ touches this water, the bridegroom touches our death, our lack of love, our poverty, our inability to love, our fear to love, and changes it into new love. As Adam explains, "a new love could begin only through a meeting with the Bridegroom."

Christ "the Bridegroom" brings about new wine, the best wine, a wine the couple has never, ever tasted beforehand, because it comes from him, it is *Christ's Love*. Christ alone can give Anna a new love for Stefan. As Adam says: *"to love means to give life through death"*, and the only one who has loved the enemy by dying is Christ, and his love has risen from death.

Anchor your love to *Love*

At the end of the play, Adam explains the true meaning of spousal *love*:

> Love is not an adventure. It has the flavour of the whole man. *It has his weight and the weight of his whole fate.* It cannot be a single moment. Man's eternity passes through it. *That is why it is to be found in the dimensions of God, because only God is eternity.*

Love carries people away like an absolute, although it lacks absolute dimensions. But acting under an illusion, they do not try to anchor that love to the Love that has such a dimension. They do not even feel the need, blinded as they are not so much by the force of their emotion as by the lack of humility. They lack humility towards what love must be in its true essence.

Anna and Stefan, the married couple at Cana, every married couple need to meet "the Bridegroom", need an encounter with Jesus Christ and his love for us.

This encounter happens in humility, having recognised that *'we can't'...we cannot* turn water into wine, *we cannot* forgive, *we cannot* turn the other cheek, *we cannot* bring life from death, we are afraid of loving to the point of death. That is the hour when the "Bridegroom" comes.

Love – says Adam at the end of Wojtyla's play – is the ultimate sense of our lives. Every married couple needs to *anchor their love to Love*. The shape of this anchor is the shape of the cross, its weight is the weight of the cross. The sufferings in your marriage, your incapacity to forgive the other, your fear of facing the other, your lack of love – in one word, your cross – is exactly this anchor which makes you hold on to Christ and his *Love,* and makes your marriage transcend the dimension of *amor* (human love) and reach the dimension of *caritas* (God's love).

7.

From Shunem to Emmaus

"The domestic Church"

The last 'word' on marriage is in fact two words: Shunem and Emmaus. These are two places, two villages, mentioned in the Bible; Shunem in the Old Testament and Emmaus in the New Testament. In these two villages God visits a married couple, transforming their lives.

Shunem: the domestic Church

Shunem is a small village mentioned in the Book of the Kings, situated in the northern territory of Israel. In this village lives a wealthy married couple of prominent social status. They are very hospitable, the door of their house is open to the stranger and the poor. They are a devoted and religious couple.

Chapter four of the Second Book of the Kings (vv. 8-17) describes how the relationship of this married couple with the prophet Elisha evolves. At first, we may say, it looks very much like a Sunday Mass relationship. This couple enjoys the presence of the prophet on a regular basis, they look forward to his company, they love hearing his voice, listening to the Word of God, and sharing a meal with him. This married couple has a faithful Sunday Mass relationship. But at one moment, perhaps after many years, something changes. They need a more stable relationship, they want more of the prophet, the Sunday visit is not enough any more:

> One day Elisha was passing through Shunem, where a wealthy woman lived, who urged him to have a meal. So whenever he passed that way, he would stop there for a meal. She said to her husband, "Look, I am sure that this man who regularly passes our way is a holy man of God. Let us make a small roof chamber with walls, and put there for him a bed, a table, a chair, and a lamp, so that he can stay there whenever he comes to us." (vv. 8-10)

What this couple is saying to God is *'stay with us'*, there is a place for you in our house, there is a room for you in our family, we need you to remain with us. In the words of the woman a room "with walls". This sounds like a simple narrative detail, but it is much more. They could have provided a tent for this man of God, and still been extremely hospitable and kind. But this is not about mercy and hospitality; this married couple wants to build up a new stable relationship with God, and to do this they need to set up permanent walls made of solid bricks and stones. To build a wall takes time, demands attention, money, care, work. We can imagine an oratory, a prayer room, a sort of chapel, simple but beautifully decorated, ready for the presence of God.

You may think this is excessive, but what this couple is saying is that the Sunday Mass visit, or a temporary accommodation, is not enough for them. They need a solid and permanent space for God in their marriage. Moreover, we read in the text that it is a "roof chamber", that is an upper room, the best part of the house, where there is more sunlight and ventilation. Why are they doing all of this?

> One day when he came there, he went up to the chamber and lay down there. He said to his servant Gehazi, "Call the Shunammite woman." When he had called her, she stood before him. He said to him, "Say to her, 'Since you have taken all this trouble for us, what may be done for you? Would you have a word spoken on your behalf to the king or to the commander of the army?'" She answered, "I live among my own people." He said, "What then may be done for her?" Gehazi answered, "Well, she has no son, and her husband is old."
> (vv. 11-14)

This married couple has a great suffering, they have no son, no children. She is the last of the barren women of the Old Testament. In the biblical world being barren is not so much a problem of fertility, but an existential suffering equalled to death. And maybe your marriage too has lost its life, you too are experiencing a deep suffering, your marriage too is somehow dead.

It is inside this form of death that the prophet Elisha enters, the living Word of God. The dialogue between the married couple of Shunem and the prophet is around their death. A dialogue initiated by God – it is the prophet himself who calls her up – and a dialogue "at the door" – it is the woman who knocks. Listening to the Word of God, standing at the door, dialoguing with the Word of God, this couple discovers that the Word of God is alive and powerful. God makes promises and fulfils them, and he alone can change death into life, can bring out new life from a situation of death.

> He said, "Call her." When he had called her, she stood at the door. He said, "At this season, in due time, you shall embrace a son." She replied, "No, my lord, O man of God; do not deceive your servant."
>
> The woman conceived and bore a son at that season, in due time, as Elisha had declared to her. (vv. 15-17)

The house of this family from Shunem has become like a small church in miniature. This barren woman and her old husband by building an upper room made of walls are in fact building a 'domestic Church' to welcome the saving presence of God. Their married life marked by death is visited by the Word of God and in the dialogue with this Word – within the walls of a domestic Church – the marriage is completely transformed and has become the place for new life.

A Christian marriage is this 'domestic church' where man and woman, wife and husband, are not any longer only two, but they have made room for a third person: woman, man, and the living Word of God, Jesus Christ.

Emmaus: catechumenate and family in mission

Emmaus is the name of a village mentioned in chapter twenty four of the Gospel of Luke. This very well-known passage (*Lk* 24:13-35) tells the journey of two of Christ's disciples journeying to Emmaus on the evening of the day of the Resurrection. Weighed down with sadness, faces cast low; the two are on their way home having lost all hopes and full of disappointments. Of these two disciples we only know the name of one – Cleopas. There is no reason not to think of them as a married couple, or even a couple engaged to be married. This couple is going through a moment of darkness, maybe oppressed by fears about the future, or questions they cannot answer. Their spirit is clouded, and their married life has lost joy and hope. Along their way, something happens: 'the two become three', and things begin to change! A stranger begins walking alongside them, not saying many words, not asking questions, simply accompanying them on their journey.

> Now on that same day two of them were going to a village called Emmaus, about seven miles from Jerusalem, and talking with each other about all these things that had happened. While they were talking

and discussing, Jesus himself came near and went with them, but their eyes were kept from recognising him. And he said to them, "What are you discussing with each other while you walk along?" They stood still, looking sad. Then one of them, whose name was Cleopas, answered him, "Are you the only stranger in Jerusalem who does not know the things that have taken place there in these days?" He asked them, "What things?" They replied, "The things about Jesus of Nazareth, who was a prophet mighty in deed and word before God and all the people, and how our chief priests and leaders handed him over to be condemned to death and crucified him. But we had hoped that he was the one to redeem Israel. Yes, and besides all this, it is now the third day since these things took place. Moreover, some women of our group astounded us. They were at the tomb early this morning, and when they did not find his body there, they came back and told us that they had indeed seen a vision of angels who said that he was alive. Some of those who were with us went to the tomb and found it just as the women had said; but they did not see him." (vv. 13-24)

Speaking to parish priests gathered in Rome, Pope Francis spoke of "the need for a true catechumenate for the Sacrament of Matrimony", recommending "the implementation of a true catechumenate of future spouses including all the steps of the sacramental path:

time of preparation for the marriage, its celebration and the years immediately after."[30] What the 'stranger' in this Gospel is doing with the two married or engaged disciples is in fact a 'catechumenate', meaning a journey of initiation, a sort of long school of Christianity, "that demands an individual's whole strength, mind, will and heart...which is itself not merely a process of intellectual instruction but, above all, a process of conversion."[31] The heart of this marriage changes – converts – around 'two tables' – we can say – the "table of the Word of God" and the "table of the Eucharist", where both the Word and the Bread are broken up.[32]

> Then he said to them, "Oh, how foolish you are, and how slow of heart to believe all that the prophets have declared! Was it not necessary that the Messiah should suffer these things and then enter into his glory?" Then beginning with Moses and all the prophets, he interpreted to them the things about himself in all the scriptures.
>
> As they came near the village to which they were going, he walked ahead as if he were going on.

---

[30] Pope Francis to participants in the course on the marriage process, 25 February 2017. Addressing the Tribunal of the Roman Rota on 29 January 2018, Pope Francis recommended a permanent "*marriage catechumenate*, intended as an indispensable itinerary for young people and couples".

[31] Pope Benedict XVI, Joseph Ratzinger, *Principles of Catholic Theology*, Ignatius Press, 1987, p. 35.

[32] Pope John Paul II, Apostolic letter *Mane Nobiscum Domine*, §§ 12 and 13.

But they urged him strongly, saying, "Stay with us, because it is almost evening and the day is now nearly over." So he went in to stay with them. When he was at the table with them, he took bread, blessed and broke it, and gave it to them. Then their eyes were opened, and they recognised him; and he vanished from their sight. They said to each other, "Were not our hearts burning within us while he was talking to us on the road, while he was opening the scriptures to us?" (vv. 25-32)

"Stay with us, Lord, for it is almost evening" (cf. *Lk* 24:29). This was the invitation that the two married disciples journeying to Emmaus on the evening of the day of the Resurrection addressed to this stranger who had accompanied them on their journey. "Stay with us" and – we continue to read – *"he went in to stay with them"*. These words are one of the most beautiful expressions we find in the New Testament about Christian marriage: *"with us"* – not solely two, but husband and wife with Christ.

The visit of Christ, the presence of Christ in this marriage not only changes the heart of the couple and opens their eyes, it changes the whole direction of their marriage!

That same hour they got up and returned to Jerusalem; and they found the eleven and their companions gathered together. They were saying, "The Lord has risen indeed, and he has appeared to Simon!" Then they told what had happened on the road, and how he had been made known to them in the breaking of the bread. (vv. 33-35)

After their 'catechumenate' on the way to Emmaus, husband and wife can return to the world, carrying now with themselves an announcement, the Good News – *"the Lord has risen indeed!"* (cf. *Lk* 24:35). Husband and wife have become "missionary disciples", and their family is now a 'family in mission'.[33]

Shunem and Emmaus, two images of the Christian family as domestic Church, where the presence of Christ in the house, with husband and wife, changes 'death' into new life and sadness into joy, opening the way to the new evangelisation. Speaking about the new evangelisation at his last Wednesday catechesis on the family, Pope Francis said how the "same familial bonds, within the experience of faith and of the love of God, are transformed, they become 'filled' with greater meaning and become capable of *going beyond themselves*."[34]

---

[33] Pope Francis, Apostolic Exhortation, *Evangelium Gaudium*, §§ 119-121; Synod Of Bishops, XIII Ordinary General Assembly, "The New Evangelization for the Transmission of the Christian Faith", *Instrumentum Laboris*, 2012.

[34] Pope Francis, General Audience, 2nd September 2015.

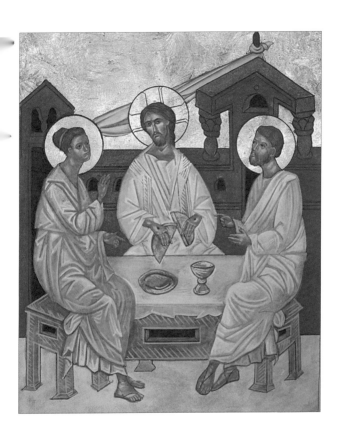

Prayer of Consecration to
the Most Sacred Heart of Jesus

Blessed are You Lord God, Eternal Father.

Our marriage comes from your goodness to us,
You are the one who brought us together
and leads our life.

We place the Most Sacred Heart of your Son Jesus
at the centre of our marriage:
a heart free from sin
a heart giving to the other
a heart burning of love
a heart open to the will of God

Dispel from our marriage Satan our enemy, the spirit
of evil, and send your healing remedy, the Archangel
Raphael, to guide us and defend us.

Amen